# Schism Blue

CHRISTINA TUDOR-SIDERI

# Schism
# Blue

*an object by*
**SUBLUNARY EDITIONS**
*of Seattle, WA*

# SCHISM BLUE

This book is our etymology. Is the reading of the most precious body, which nowadays cannot be found, of this Most Near man whom I do not await whom I await on the other re-embroidered side of time.

HÉLÈNE CIXOUS, *TOMB(E)*; TR. LAURENT MILESI

And I begin again to scrape, to scratch, to dredge the bottom of the sea [...] I barely hear the noise of the water from the little room.

JACQUES DERRIDA, *GLAS*;<br>TR. JOHN P. LEAVEY, JR. & RICHARD RAND

*In and of itself, a moment is also its interpretation. An image, psychologically, philosophically, at the intersection of sense and mind, is also its own absence. An image, positioned in the foreground, not for emphasis, but to be erased—to be erased and recast as shape, as form, as flesh. An essentially reversible concept, a chiastic structure that moves the body inasmuch as it fills the eye. Across the coastline, across the skin, a line like an extension of the soul, offered to other souls, other images, other bodies; a fragment of consciousness like a hand behind one's back, empty and at the same time brimming with representation. A line tantalizing the furthest limits of the visible. I could start with a here-and-now, with a sequence of events. This world comes, after all, from the tradition of doing just so. If a symposium were to be organized, something formal, something obliging, a discussion around the motifs of one's relation to the past, perhaps I could address then the unity of bodies in their passage through time. I could make*

*a montage out of identity and ruin and still-frames sutured to
the awareness of absence, out of the figure of the lover and the
chaos that passed through the body not in orgasm but through
the body in pain; a montage out of the utterly slow dislocation
of this progressive loss of contact, of touch, this solidified
climax which could only be measured in the embryonic form
that no longer is. But when intimate, when struggling, when
breathing with difficulty, when moving, in a haste, toward a
landscape that is neither psychological or philosophical, nor
in need of auto-affections, when tempted by the apocalyptic
refusal of time to grant another hour, that is when the union
remains one of exteriority, in that no fitting motif could be
traced from within, no mark could be exposed and no account
constructed. If I am outside, if I touch the greenery of seasons
to come, with the mind, with the senses, with the nakedness of
the body as page, with the blankness of the page as body, I
think then that I exist, even if as the fabric of an idea—an
idea, material, wrapping itself around the skull—and that is
how I write, that is how I now travel the length of moments
from where I gather ink and dreams and envelopes and words
to seal within. That is how the self becomes pure possibility;
and water, and sand, and elemental love. That is how the I
that exists renders distance impossible. That is how I am able
to utter: I exist, I possess this body, I reinvent the vestige of
reinvention itself. Truth is in the skin, but the measure that
defines it knows no corporeal limit. Furthermore: I reinvent
the spectator, in this life and in all others, time and time*

*again, until no flower and no fiber resemble another, for that is how one weaves together the sense of being. Dare I provide such instruments of torment? Dare my hand defile the memory of his immediacy? There are ways to throw one's arms around each moment, ways to relive and put to sleep each death, each birth, each recollection. Ways to fall in a swoon and ways to enter the city of one's final hour. I hold between my fingers a phenomenology not of experience, but of performance. Remember that. I submerge my fingers in a blue not of the sea, nor of the sky, but a blue of the wintriest of hearts. Through this decantation, I survive the catastrophe. Between my mouth and my voice, between any mouth and any voice, the whole of the world balances itself like a trembling leaf on the cross of its decay. Through this reinvention, through this projection of my own desire, I erase the body and the self. Through this intertextual fulfillment, I conjure the wonderful fantasy of putting my hands around death's throat. I plunge in and out of details, I draw parallels, I transform myself into crisis, and temporality, and poem. I do it all for a return, an indentation, a celebration of image as keeper of life. I become the written corpus of the world and I allow misreading and touch and narrativization. Through this commitment to the Other, through the erotics of this sublimation, through this writing outside the frame, I myself become another. There are ways to put to sleep each death. There are ways to bring back to life each rapture. There are ways.*

Out of his rotting body trees and flowers grow,
and he is in them, and that is eternity.

IN THE HALF-LIGHT, in the dark, nowhere. To let the world end here: what inconceivable pleasure. To speak no more, to write no more, to give way for the eye to see, to allow it to travel through time, back-and-forth, to let the eye see everything but the present moment. To let the eye see her: drawing, devoting herself to a life of projection and symbol and reproduction. To let it cast its gaze over the lines she is veiling with the movement of her hands, the contours of a house; no, the crown of a forest, the waves of a sea, the relics of a city; branches and waves and arteries like strands of hair flowing from one world into another, from love into death, from hands rummaging through the past as if it were the heart of hearts into the gulf of all blue, the blue of horizons and the blue of crossings over the ocean of time.

To let the eye see her: exposed, wicked, determined; to see her and become an object under the spell of her lines and circles; to see her and come back to life minutes before whatever she has planned is about to unravel.

To let the world end here, before the narrow room is ever created, before there is paint on the walls and on her fingers, before there is silk on the bed, before philosophical thought rooted in reason entangles itself with the mythological, before imagination and desire and grief expand to absurd lengths—the grief that brings everything into existence—before the tenets of separation are ever given any names: what inconceivable pleasure.

The stage is empty and silent. There are lights, yes; lights that loom over all vacancies, from high above, lights like memories of transit, lights tied away from the judgment of the viewer; lights in bondage, lights no longer radiant to the eye of the current spectator. There are lights, but one can only see in darkness. She knows that reality can only be entered through this darkness.

Five days have passed since the first snow of the year. Days when lips were silent, days engulfed in impossibility, days like obligations, like woes, like manners of living, days vilified, unhappy; days like souls abased. During this time, all she managed to do was hide behind the dark of her eyelids.

In the distance, in this image of time past, separated by flowing lines: two humans, two characters, two opposing shades, two different perspectives, the real and the recreated; his hand in the color of her body, fire at the root.

A sublime image. A submission to form, to ways of being in the eyes of another; eroticized, paradoxical, thematic. Thematic, yes, for the representation of this separation lies at the core of everything.

Between them, the night, its shadows, ambivalent as to whom to protect, him or her; the night that cannot tear itself asunder, the night that cannot offer itself to both of them; the night, its shadows in disarray, from her steps to his hesitations and back again, from the idea, no, from the essence of a god, the god of this painting in reverse, this painting that shows her leaving when it was, in fact, that reality took the shape of his departure; from this essence of a god to the rest of the world, in throes, to the world immersed in petty passions and ebbing desires and folding of the senses.

And everywhere, these shadows; from him to her, eternally so. These shadows, circumstantial brushstrokes of improbable precision.

Black silhouettes and incandescent patterns of white draw the eye away from its wandering gaze. The past vanishes as if it was never anywhere but in a mind that no longer remembers it. Nothing but the artifact of this mind. No here and there, no then and now, no near and far. The stage is now a cemetery. The body in the coffin is covered in snow, but for a scar on the left hand, right below the index finger, a line of white traversing the mauve of mourning, like a wound on the canvas of a painting soon-to-be-covered by the white gesso of new creations.

How many hours must pass? The thought comes while gazing absentmindedly in the distance, further, far beyond what lies before her. It comes with no distinction other than the fictional, that which she gathered from books, and films, and from the lives of others. How much snow must fall for the hand to be buried with the body?

The sequence of events, what those attending were asked not to call a funeral, but a farewell, unravels with the indolence of a winter fire. Fire that feels permanent and yet passes in the blink of an eye. The spellbound eye traveling back-and-forth through time. And look, the farewell, too, has passed.

One could speak here about performances and role reversals, about the theater as playground of the imagination or the stage as a manifestation of memory; one could speak about the alternating soft and hard, cold and warm body and its capacity for martyrdom, for dance, for literature, for coming into and out of the sea. One could speak, but the pretext of nonlinearity demands a departure from this vague scene, from this death, from the indulgence of this tissue that snow will not touch.

White space falls from the sky and separates one

moment from another, one memory from another, one life from another. White space as a propaedeutic model for recreation.

Minutes later, hours later, in another intermission, under the careful gaze of the eye, they are walking home. She is walking ahead of him, to allow his thoughts generous space for a return. A gathering of all that troubles his mind, above the body, above the head, outside of it, like a meandering cloud drawn by the eager hand of a child on a random afternoon; a horizontal spasm manifesting inside a moment when the eye has traveled so far back that it has pierced the skin and deafened the ear.

I am waiting for you. A crucial whisper, an echo, directed at the one who can no longer hear.

This exercise in reconstruction, elaborate and demanding, this attempt at birthing enough chaos as to mask the natural sequence of events—she planned this for months in advance, from before even knowing, from when she first felt it; before meeting him; from when it came to her that one day she will speak of a *body of work* and that body will be a real body, one that she will recreate with her very hands; an actual, living, breathing, loving body.

Her desire was to become more and more intense with the passing of time, to the point that there were nights when she would find herself walking the streets just to find this body, just to come face to face with this person whom she could later bring back to life. Nights when she would linger outside of theaters, bars, cinemas, ordinary buildings, thinking herself a kind of textual disorder, an illness on the page, a malformation, even, in the book of time, a narrative that should not have been written, but since she had been given this path, the exigency of this path, there was now no alternative but to walk it. And this walk is what is staged here.

Somewhere, anywhere, everywhere, unnamed, unencountered, him—this body, still to come, her first page, her first circle, a taxonomy of touch, the immediate site of sex and sorrow and escapism, the site of crossings and course corrections and immortality.

Contemplating this hereafter, she felt like a god punished to live no other life than the one afforded by the animation of her creation.

One night, minutes before midnight, around the corner from a small theater that she did not normally frequent, exiting a play about the nature of wasted life, there he was, this body, the revenant subject of her coming inhumanities.

That was the night she decided to let herself be devoured.

Years later, outside the frame, in the cemetery, snow falls as if to be given a voice and speak of blood, as if to place above a blanket of white and echoes, a blanket under which one body is permitted to resemble another. For her, this is precisely what must not happen, she is not ready, familiarity must not resettle, the old must not reemerge, not until she has planned its rebirth herself.

The blanket falls, nonetheless, until one mind is able to provide breath for another. A phantom possibility. A blanket of ice above the decomposition of organs in the body.

In thinking of the world through the white of the sky, she restricts herself to space and to how light falls upon it. To light that chases its own course.

There is no black snow in our world; a thought she attributes also to the presence of light. To light and how it falls and how it abandons itself to the space that welcomes it, how it envelops and makes visible; to light and how it erases the outlines and configurations of this very space; to how it pushes everything beyond the soul that lingers; how it learns and eagerly waits for any and all forms of annihilation, for destruction and delusion to show themselves through the reappearance of all that is lost.

While she herself is waiting; while she is walking, and writing, and planning; while she asks herself whether the death of the ego is the same as the death of the self, for she has to clean herself of all traces of present oneness, she has to scrub away its skin from atop her skin, she asks also whether in creating another, in recreating another—the Other—she might perhaps find new possibilities of being, which she considers in itself a critique of all questions, an arrow cast in the direction of all matters of epistemology. An alignment with aesthetics and semiotics and the cinematic image of unconsciousness.

Further, if it were to be just so, if such a transformation were to occur, she asks herself, What role would identity then play, and how far back in the past must she return in order to find it? But this, most of all this: What role would identity play in the time it takes for light to fall as snow from the sky and bury the scarring of the hand?

There might be another way to grasp it. There are always other ways. One could peek inside her mind; one could pull back the hair from her eyes as if pulling back a heavy curtain, and find there this erethism, find in the dark of her eyes the over-faithful reinvention she ardently craves.

To birth anew a couple. Words that come as if to provide an answer for this question that has settled like a veil over her eyes, this question from nowhere; words that come as if to set free a solution, to release it into the space of paths ahead.

A passage through the mirror. A splintered dialogue between the two sides of the same face, between the two halves of the same body. A dialogue inviting creation. Justifying it. A dialogue fleshing out the contours of the mind. Two human beings, appearing for the first time as to always appear, in the half-light, in the dark, nowhere.

She seeks to birth anew two humans, deprived of seduction and illusion and denial. Deprived in order to recapture new instances of each and every event, to recapture enjoyment and voluptuousness and insatiable satisfaction. She seeks to transfer the lost, as simple as with a carbon copy. To birth anew and to revoice these humans inside a space that reveals nothing but the very notion of existence, inside a space that does not inform them of their past, a space that, through no matter what connection, teaches and guides them along this thought, this idea, and later, this forgetting of themselves, and perhaps then, to have them utter definitions of what one truly calls ego, and love, and death, and all that rests at the foot of the bed: the unexamined, the unlived, the unremembered—to utter all that has become a concept, to speak of the ego in the absence of that which tames it, even though they will both live there, here, always facing each other, one the mirror of the other; as one world ends, and another, reinvented, created, imagined, grows to touch the hand of the eternal.

To have them utter, furthermore, the why—why, in this resurrection, they have not seen that the narrow room, the room in which resides the whole of their world, resembles the one they themselves once inhabited, when alive, when real, when original. To utter all this, impossible to find in themselves, impossible to carry within in the absence of memory, yet to utter it nonetheless, for how else could she justify this reawakening if not through the importance of finding each other in spite of memory, in spite of living flesh, in spite of the funereal space that has taken over each corner of the world?

They are in the room now, almost complete, almost drawn to the scope of their fullness. They address and dissect and write their findings with chalk on the floor even though a little something is still missing from the body of each. They write with black ink in journals that she meticulously placed amidst the blue for them to fill.

An ability they must have had before, from the first moment, from their first encounter, from that night outside of the theater, since their writing, performed in such a way, in stages and everywhere at once, is primordial to what she needs them to rebecome. They are here now, and they write that to live is not to suffer, but rather, to live is to become a symbol of yearning. To live is to be mise-en-scène and imprudence and wetness against the backcloth of abandonment.

Typographically, for one could say that they are a book, the pages of a book awaiting to be bound together, they are dark orgasm and textual dimension and the consummation —the reconsummation—of a life as object, an object shattered by the hand of time. This is how they should be understood. This is their primary manifestation: as text that comes and passes beyond its limits. As text that haunts; toward the Other, in the Other. As text. As body. As world and being-in-the-world.

Chronologically, and it bears mentioning that chronology would ground her in impossibility, therefore, however she is to draw it, however she is to write it, from whatever moment one—anyone—were to enter and acquaint themselves with this process, it would all make perfect sense: these are nothing but glimpses of life and methods of recreating them. Symptoms of tenderness through the veins.

These are replays and relocations, and through them all runs a relinquishment of the chronological.

Even so, the eye wanders, and in its wandering, it seems to have reached a starting point.


But to write of their abrupt beginning is to admit that an onset was needed, it is to say: yes, a framework of flesh and blood was necessary. Something, someone, through whom thought can pass and circle itself, and then circle them, for the circle always closes, while the door to the narrow room never opens, and in doing so, the circle, that is, captures within not the explanation of why there had to be people, human beings walking from one corner of the narrow room to the other, always facing each other, confined to this tight space, of why she needed them and could not simply write or speak or draw mere concepts, mere memories, mere representations of what was once real, of why she needed to fill the space with breath instead of remembrance—when the circle closes, it captures within its closure the very need for clarification. An action at once scornful and enigmatical. An ontological devouring.

Inconsistent, even. A remark that comes from her, as she dips her fingers in more ink and smiles at this thought, that something as the closing of a circle can ever be inconsistent.

To let the world end here, on this street, in this tunnel, amidst these darkening waves, in this assimilation, in the infinite action of this absorption, embraced by this death, by this tyrannical need that pours down from the sky; to let water flood the very mouth conjuring this tale; to preserve nothing more, nothing than the eye that wanders and sees and gets lost in what it captures on its journey; to let the world end here: what inconceivable pleasure.

I COULD BE THE WIND, he often uttered to himself at night. Loud enough for someone to hear him, if someone were to pass through, if someone were to already be there, in the room with him, at night, when these thoughts would come, these regrets at having left, at having returned, these strange omissions of the mind, for in thinking them, he no longer remembered life, but rather a simulation of it. Yes, I could travel, and embrace, and return; always return at the right moment, without shame, without deceit, always return to touch her face on winter mornings. A vain display of affection that when it happened nonetheless warmed her for days to come. A kindness, like a continuous effervescence, vibrancy and life and fire from within; something that kept on boiling inside both of them, even though at the root lingered this distinction that they had chosen to ignore; even though at the root, laced there, was the confusion of still life. I could be the wind. I could travel. I could return.

But nothing must truly be uttered, not anymore, and so his thoughts remained trapped inside a reality that never was, a hallucinatory unreality, a phenomenological reduction of both reality and unreality; they remained trapped under the untouched skin, in the movement of fingers and in the flight of birds outside the windows of other lives. Trapped inside the excess of nonbeing.

Nothing must be uttered, nothing more than questions, all the questions to come, crammed inside a single one, inside the only question possible, the question that utters its own erasure, its own futility; everything in this one construction: interrogation, demand, doubt, anything that the mind imagined for itself as a kind of attempt at escaping the body when it went out looking for answers and the possibility of escape gained a certain glow bestowed by the existence of the sun, and other people, and waters at the edge of the city; when the body walked and walked and these questions accumulated inside like malignant tumors—like tumors, these questions directed at someone, at anyone, at what remains when one walks out of the theater at night and the stage changes in absentia, and there, just around the corner, there is this body, hers, and there are the hands of this body, hands already in mourning, hands already cold, hands unreadable, hands like images on the walls of museums and cathedrals from time past.

Questions directed at those meant to chronicle this very moment, in the mind, in the air, in the tunnel, in all the tunnels of life, the moment when, fully synchronized, two humans, one the gentle half of the other; the lonely ones, the only ones, stood facing each other for enough time as to know that mortality was but a word that their breath could erase in an instant.

How strange to speak, he thought. When he touched her, when he wrote, when night fell upon the eyelids of the day; when hope and honesty and frantic love disentangled themselves just before falling into the rarely kind embrace of sleep.

How strange to speak, to use dark words, to use long words.

He was nine years old when he first discovered that he harbored an interest in the slippage of time. He would close his eyes and envision the asymmetrical melting clock. Slippage, that is just what his child-mind called it, for he found it amusing, as if one were holding a small, slippery fish, as if one were returning to the river its offspring, by accident. A still-frame like the one he saw in documentaries: boy and creature and river passing through. Slippage, like the confusion of a warm embrace that hugs the body too tightly, like an adumbration of the self, a perspective of being once a child, in love with love itself, captivated; dis-covering, losing from his small hands the very time that he will regain years later, in the narrow room; time like a second shadow of the self; time like the experience of all senses; time like the worth of things; time like pretense, even, a pretense of temporal implication and schisms to come; a pretense of running, without a body, without food, without forgiveness, running through regions of ink and ruin.

He loved dearly this slippage of time; he loved to look up and wonder, in cathedrals, in museums, in the attic of his family's small house; wonder in what manner time touches upon the self; to look up in search of a possible answer and capture murals with the eye of the mind, to imagine and pretend and replace what was real with celestial spheres and ruptures of paradise.

A canvas he painted for himself and himself alone, hidden from everyone else; something of emotive value, something that would later reemerge in the drawings and writings that were to bring him back to life. An answer for questions to come. Desire as continuity.

Sometimes, when the sky was too black for him to see the very seconds of time resting upon the clouds, he would turn his attention to the ground, and would search there for what the blue no longer offered. For a renewal of murmurs and appetite and beautiful transgressions. He would lower his gaze and search there for the natural course of his beautifully-painted world.

He would walk like that, head to the ground, for miles and miles, circling the neighborhood, sometimes getting lost, sometimes stumbling, sometimes kicking rocks in anger, other times realizing that he had only moved a few steps.

And there, amidst passion flowers and sand and grass and snakes that crawled eager to chain his little feet in their slithering, he saw the years, he saw life and the paths he could take; he saw love, and literature, and possibility, he saw riches only he desired, and so they would always be abundant.

He saw all this how the lover sees the world: connected, enthralled, charmed, he saw them transcending the particularities of the physical body; and even though he did not understand, he saw also an immense darkness, which, at the time, he took to be the mirroring of the sky above.

When he got older and began to understand that what resided at his feet and high up in the sky of his childhood was nothing like that which life was to present him with, not even like the question of silence; nothing like the zero absolutes of his youth, like the despondency of his early twenties, when the inevitability of death, his death or anyone's, and the threat of a wasted life clouded his mind such that no refuge was left for the eye, that no means of communication was left for the mouth; that is when he no longer knew how to refer to himself as someone human. Imagine, he would say to himself—Imagine: a ghost. A haunting. Materiality and body as make-believe. Imagine: the unreality of the body passing through life as hours through time.

Was his life before nothing but artifice? Was his childhood a sort of preexistence in the garden of Eden? Had there been too many interventions, too many modifications, too many alterations to life as he once discovered it? Where would he even look in order to question the nature of existence? Of his existence. At the corporeal, the emotional, the synthesis of the two? At the experienced? At touch? He looked at touch—he made of it a deconstruction, from it, he opened and closed himself to all that was lost, to all that he might have wished to regain, if he were to ever feel human again. Undoing the discretion of touch, unmarking and rechanging its meaning, making of it now a proposition, something to offer the mind as to quiet it, something to give thought in order not to tangle itself in this web of darkness that had fallen and captured him. It is only the human who can think, he repeated to himself over and over. Only the human who can feel. And so, through symptoms and wounds and absences, because of them, he allowed himself to embrace the new. Through all of this, language was always there. Language as silence, language as gaze, language in lieu of the gaping mouth, language as witness. Language before image. He read, and learned, and listened, and from all this, he took but one reality: we are in a state of anguish. A profound responsibility—not that of becoming, of being a flower, like he had read in the poems of his childhood, but the responsibility to be anything; to be in a state of anguish. To be.

For a while, he did not know, he could not isolate the meaning of this *we* and as much as he struggled, he had no idea whether it was that of the self, the collection that harbors all selves—but no, that would be too individualistic, it would mean to deny the existence of others in ways different than the ones of his early years, when he would paint for himself and for himself alone—or that of the world, of all beings and objects and trees that sway with the wind.

Whatever it was, however it came to him, it remained clear, this catastrophic bearing: that there was anguish, and awareness, and mental suffering that he could not find explanation for; panic and despair whereby he would lose all trust in the world as it came to him; all trust, in the morning and at midnight; in the world as it would present itself, when one night, walking home from the theater, he would be given the possibility of being reborn. The possibility of being rewritten and reread in accordance with the laws of eternity.

The undulating shoreline extended toward the left of his body, while the moon was reflected in the water of this unknown sea, of these waves that he was visiting for the first time. Holding his head in his palm, pensive, as if posing for one of his paintings, he thought of how easy it would be to become one with what no longer is. Not to drown, not to walk into the sea, but simply to vanish, right then and there, without knowing it, as he was standing on the sea-facing rock; to vanish without effort, even without thought, for thinking about such matters left him feeling guilty and embarrassed and humiliated by this ability he had of removing himself from the world without ever considering that his body warms the bodies of others. To vanish like a helpless prey. To become the one no longer in need of touch. To vanish in the softness of nonbeing.

How easy it would be to end, here, in front of the sea that reflects the moon, how easy it would be to break with his destructive nature, in which, paradoxically, he always found great comfort; how easy to free himself of thoughts that, after all, are nothing but this: insufficient thoughts, skimpy, extinguishable; and how easy to free himself of what these thoughts hide, of what they conceal, that is, of his inability of acting upon any of these torments. Nothing is less certain than these thoughts.

But no, he did not regret his weakness, nor did he see it as such, he did not desire death, what he longed for, ever since he became aware that these matters existed, from the first time he looked up inside a cathedral and no longer saw the wonderful murals of childhood, was to act—it was life he desired, life he wished to embrace, life that would come and build itself in front of him from the slivers of his actions, from his movements and from his touches.

People must decide, he read somewhere, no longer remembering now what it was that they must decide on. But yes, people must decide, and he too was there, in front of the undulating shoreline, because he had to decide, but upon remembering, briefly, from where this need for a decision rose, the inexplicable contradiction of this need, he got up and returned to his room as if to mark through this gesture the end of his desire for movement and decision and whatever acts of life depended on him.

During that night, he thought of nothing, he banished from his mind any trace of belief and want and action, he exiled the very studies on choice in which he had immersed himself weeks before, he brushed aside theory and urge and demand, he forgot all about performance, and consequence, and even empirical investigation, giving himself to the tremors of his body, without recognizing in them what kept coming and what was to come.

Now, in the final year of his life, time no longer appears

to be slipping. Time has already passed, and he felt, in these resounding months, as if he were living someone else's time; as if he were wearing someone else's watch and counting someone else's seconds; as if he had somehow found a way to go on living after death, since to him death came and took the mind in the moment of its first fall, when the body first uttered: I am frail, and the mind knew, from then on, that no eternity was possible.

He had lived on someone else's time ever since, and this living, this life that coursed through his veins, this life gave him more than any of his real seconds ever gave him; and with it, through it, the realization that time passed in vain when it belonged to him, when it came and gave him the world but he did not take it, for there will always be, he thought at the time, there will always be other lives and there will always be onedays and maybes and possibilities so infinite that he could grab none.

DARKNESS FALLS AND THE PAGE IS ANOTHER, the hour is another, the room is inhabited yet again, and even though there is no longer a need for it, even though the perfection of the soul has been achieved, she keeps on writing, and walking, and planning. She keeps on writing but writing is not writing as the world knows it, the words are not formed on the page as hands are meant to form them, but rather they appear in chalk on the floor, in ink on the walls and in the air; and it is not always clear whether they do so by way of hands, if they were always there, or if, and that is something that the cross-textual nature of a life together might explain better than anything else, the nature of the opening to the Other, if the words are materializing from collisions and uncertainties, from mechanical praxis and the manner in which touch inscribes something on the body, something overwhelmingly intense, something so radical that no linguistic representation is possible, and in it there are words like extensions of potentiality. Regardless, writing is what they have always called it, and she must honor it such as the mind remembers it, a bearing into the brain, this act of living, of stepping into the river thought-first, this breath between them: a letter, and then another.

He reads from above, serenely awaiting his turn, undecided on whether he is to erase or add on.

She writes, and in doing so, feels as if she were sutured to the skin of the night. She writes: sometimes, on the stage, or in the street, consciousness speaks not of existence, but of mimesis. She writes: the tussle of the voice to convey the heart is nothing more than the aspiration of the self, an absence in presence, a presence in absence; an adored experience, that of attracting and being attracted to what governs everything, to knowledge by way of effort, through thinking and becoming, and always moving toward the dark, toward that which is unknown, omitted, toward the natural that one does not yet recognize as nature, toward new modalities of sight, toward tension and desire—desire for knowledge, yes, but also desire for gaining corporeality, gaining voice, gaining the ability to touch and be touched through the drive toward finding everything, discovering everything, becoming everything, and then replicating it; knowing oneself through this ascension, through this rewarding of one's efforts: the ability to hold continuous creation within the grasp of one's hand. She writes: there is no presence but presence as exposure. There is no shaping that does not foresee the shape. No demand without the demand of existence. And mimesis, this mimesis that shows itself on the stage, as if there and only there can it be protected, by the presence of an audience, as if there and only there can it pour forth to a public, this mimesis is itself an invention. Something one creates. Something one desires into being. And so it comes; it comes and annuls itself and with it the whole of the world. The world as virtue, the world as happiness, the world as two human beings, together. She writes: this structure, this essence, this ink—more for others than for ourselves; more for ourselves than for others.

Leaving aside the incalculable, leaving aside animality and instinct, and the suppression of all excess, what remains is that the voice is unable to go beyond the limits of exhaustion. The voice is unable to be voice, and in this absence of sound, in this heavy absence, lies the toppling of all coming gestures. She longs for other voices to come and speak these words. Everything must be uttered. Nothing can be uttered. She tried herself, but she stumbled and her tongue got twisted and the lips turned blue, cold, as if they had spent an eternity under a blanket of ice, which frightened her into giving up, into no longer offering her voice to this endeavor, to this attempt to feed on life while feeding life.

A traumatic denial of the self, for it was in her very nature to utter the inescapable. Something she immediately regretted, this renunciation, for it was in her voice where he found most comfort, and, How is he to rebecome if he no longer hears my voice? she thought to herself, but the sensation of ice in her lips returned, and when she touched them, her fingers turned blue, and it was thus that she broke with any attempt at speaking as she needed to speak.

Regardless of whose voice it will be, all that is to be recreated must be uttered, all that is to reappear must find a voice to make it so, and she needed the echoes to travel the length of the narrow room; louder and louder she needed voices, through the body and through the brain; words on the tongue like silhouettes of objects reflecting upon their edges and viscera the very mirror of poetic thought.

One needs… But she pauses.

No longer patient, he grabs the chalk from her hands and writes: there are two of you.

In reading this, she does not know whether he is addressing her, himself, or the world, for there are two of everything, there had to be two of everything or else nothing would have remained of him.

He writes, no longer caring if he will one day discover the truth, this version of him that lives now by virtue of her sleepless nights, no longer caring whether he, who lives because she drifted so far off, so deep into the darkness of blue that she could bring from there enough ink as to write for him an entire life, to write him for an entire life; thinking of nothing but the intimacy of this moment, when there is still chalk powder on her hands; this moment, when there are sentences on the floor that moonlight strikes just enough to provide them with an otherworldly glow.

Her mind occupied now by nothing else, she allows herself to be afraid again. This pulsation, whether mental or carnal, fear rushing through the body, through the mind, she discovers, in this, beauties that would sustain her for years to come. To travel and return and recapture from the streets outside, from the tunnels of her years, from the cathedrals of his, that feeling of absolute fear, the loss, the wintering of the soul, not because such a thing could ever happen again, now that she has gathered all ink, but simply because without it, there would be no healing in sight, and the thought alone appeared at times more menacing and tumultuous and disorienting than what it took to reach these comforting nights.

That there was no comfort in the pull of comfort plagued her more than she was willing to admit. And yet, somehow, the fact that there was no eluding the flow of time did not occur to her once.

Time remained not an enigma, but something already cannibalized. Time was what she fed on. Time was what fed on her. Time was the very substance at the core of this alchemical process. Time, like embalming fluid through the veins.

To let the world end here, in this tunnel of the mind, in this very tunnel where she now sat on the cold, damp cement, caressing the keys of an imaginary typewriter with fingers that traced not words but the movement of ghost hands before her; the hands of souls or spirits, not of bodies, never of bodies, not even of former bodies; the hands of ideas or memories that now sit quietly beside her, waiting for their turn at stroking the air once more, to let the world end here —

To capture a soul and keep it in the background of one's days, she thought, coming to her, this phrase, as something she needed to write down, as something corporeal, but not entirely: the experience of becoming spectral; if only the typewriter would not be imaginary, if only there were ink in this dream the same as it was in the narrow room — endless ink.

To let the world end here, to let endlessness, yes, fall upon the eye like an eager veil, to shift perspective and perception and let the mind and the eye and the voice that was needed but no longer present, to let them all gather these elements, the elements of one final tale, to let the hands type: a narrow room.

What inconceivable pleasure.

And yet, How strange to write, she thought. As if writing were indeed a possibility once more, as if language were to gather itself and carry on, as if no distance were to remain between her steps and his. This, when coherent, when more human than authorial, she knew still. As if no human, no deed, no touch, no imitation were to concern themselves with anything other than this sanctuary. To write. To hope. To knot and unknot. To sacrifice the body to the text. How strange to touch a collarbone and feel a word, to count vertebrae as if letters, to count letters as if snow-covered bones.

This very night, she thought, This very night has departed from the immortality of the soul, merely to live, merely to die, merely to darken.

How strange to touch endless stretches of skin and say: how long this sentence, how heavy its meaning.

At home, for there is a home — there is a home, even though the walk there is eternal, even though snow falls upon the grave, still; even though to deprive herself of the memory of this home, to eradicate the bizarreness of its proportions, would be to embrace life itself; at home, memories rushed through her as if she were just now living them, as if they were all new experiences, regardless of absence, regardless of touch or lack thereof, regardless of the ideal or the historical or the phenomenological. There, at home, memories rushed through her, invading the mind, giving it a sense of the world. A sense of life-once-lived. Memories of being at the edge of a forest. Outside of the forest. Perhaps with her back to the trees. Perhaps with her hands above her head. On her head. Perhaps with him by her side. Standing as he stood next to the undulating shoreline, head in hand, absent, darkened by clothing and thought. At home, the revenance of all memories. Memories becoming material weight, memories reshaping the fabric of the sky; memories, in the rocking chair, on summer nights; memories of him combing her hair, in solitude, in togetherness, in the moonlight. At home, the ghostly touch of the Other.

If she were to no longer remember, if she were to no longer feel compelled to travel back to this home, to this haunted home, she would find then all that life once placed at his feet, when, in childhood, he would look up and then look down, and make from this voyage of the eyes the most beautiful painting she would ever see.

But home, at home, this thought remained: the sky could break open any minute.

A thought as old as time itself. A lullaby. An engulfing obsession, which she carried within and in her arms from page to page, from street to street, from self to self. This thought that became a dream, inside a narrow room, too narrow to hold what had been lost but lingered still, too narrow for her to sit down and write, too narrow for him to get up and walk and paint; to walk from one corner of the room to another, as if traveling the length of continents, as if rediscovering the pigment of imagination; too narrow for her to accept, to understand how absence fills a room with a voraciousness that no presence would ever be able to match.

A room too narrow to contain the question, as it came, as it rolled off the tongue, as it pained her and as it dwelled in her company like an animal that bites you and for this you love them more; this question that shared her bed and sunk its teeth into her skin, this question that stabbed her despondency; this question, as she wrote, and drew, and put to work the ink she brought back from the enchanted waters of other existences; this question, posed not by the mind, but by the memory of his hands as hers went about the routine of necessary days: Can you see me yet?

She did not see him. She saw them, the lonely ones, the invented, the recreated ones; she saw them as she herself had placed them in the narrow room; she did not see him. But for the scarred hand in the cemetery, she did not see him.

A moment to reflect, to acknowledge, to touch flesh and become touched flesh in return; a moment to know why them, why this mimicry and why this room, why in rebirth, in reincarnation, in metempsychosis; why in reinvention, why are they made to speak when the other *she* no longer has a voice and the other *he* no longer has a mouth, why are they made to write and why are they to pause and reflect and relive a life already lived?

But the moment passes and the sentence goes on, invoking a young man, and a young woman, and small ships on the sea they visited just weeks away from one another. There is nothing else to observe but the flow of this sentence, nothing but the threading of these words — words that were once seconds, hours, desires, touches. Nothing but the trembling of these words, embodiments and phantoms at the same time. Nothing but to write more words, to write and through writing to burrow not toward light but toward togetherness.

A random memory, perhaps leaving something out of its very center: an error in thought, something she let happen as to convince herself that it was real, and that this *real* can again become a world, not a copy of the world, but the world itself: wave and continuum and flesh and language that one strokes as if skin.

She writes, convinced: acquiring both materiality and essence bestows upon one the compositional voice of a poet.

After all, what is most needed is a voice. But something is still missing, something is absent from the sentence, from the way she phrased it, or perhaps from how the hand wrote it. The words do not make sense. Even so, she does not push for a repair, she does not attempt an erasure.

She writes: as if, somehow, being a poem justifies anything, as if being a poem and the river of blank space that flows through the body of this poem makes it so that no meaning resides in knowledge nor in being aware of one's existence as something created and made to write again, made to breathe in such a small space that the very definition of breathing must be rewritten, such a small space that the lungs themselves must be recast.

He comes. He reads.

BETWEEN THEM, THE FUNERAL, the farewell, the impalpable otherness, the reason for wanting, for waiting, constantly, ever-growingly; the reason for summoning and imploring death, and change, and something, anything, whatever, to live inside of her, to honor and caress and ridicule with tenderness the wound and the discourse of assurance. Between them, the reason to nurture the heart into growing another heart. And then another. And another. Until her body is abundant in these little organs like streets in cobblestones. Her body, since her body alone remains, and yes, cobblestones, for she read in a book, a long time ago, she read of streets and steps and walking not toward but away from one's own heart; she read of steps on cobblestones and seashores and any other formation the feet might encounter on their path away from what lies inside the body.

It must have been a book of poetry, though she remembers the narrator speaking in prose. The narrator spoke in prose and named the streets that she was walking on; fragrant names, derogatory names, names filled with lust, genuine lust, lust that comes from primeval fires; names inspired by the people who populated them, these streets, or by the scenery that served as their decor.

Each name she remembers and each name she has forgotten, but it is from this book that she took the idea that one can never stray too far from the heart, that no matter how many streets, no matter how many corners, how many theaters, there is always, in the nearness of the escaping body, a heart, a mirror heart, a reflection of the heart one carries within, from womb to tomb, How non-sensical, she thought, this idiom, how it erases the very journey it is meant to emphasize, how it places meaning on these two wretched concepts: the beginning and the end.

The stage is now a book. A book of poetry, for that is how she thinks of reading. Understanding belongs to the world of poetry; all is poetry, and in poetry there are oh so many words hidden between its verses, words she can gather and make her own; words to summon with her ink, words with which to rebuild and rebirth and reattempt by ways of composition, words with which to trace all that lies between beginning and end. Words that know of themselves, a hitherto absent experience.

If she were to take these words, if she were to keep them for herself, to consume them, to devour them all on her own, against the consciousness that might oppose her, she might then remember where she was going when she walked ahead of him; this body, walking, reading, loving; this sea, this death-defying sea, undulating much like the shoreline of his earlier years, to the rhythm of night's darkness.

This theme, in constant repetition, waves, and darkness, and, smuggled back on boats or through whatever other means, this theme, metaphorically, in isolation, this passage to safety that she constructed for him, this reshaping of madness and fantasy and desire so tender that no other mind and no other body could ever know about the noise of the sea and the lights of the city, this desire that no other hand and again, no other body, could summon at the height of happiness.

There will not be a day in her life when she will not protect this longing. This desire, immediate, repeating itself, this plight, this dance of life; love slipping between the fingers; a text, bearing the fate of all desires and of all texts. This desire, far from absolving her atrocities, though there is no one here to judge them as such, there is no one here beyond the ones she herself has invented, the ones she has imbued with what is good and sweet, with this osmosis that no narrator would ever again be able to corrupt.

When she was a child, and this comes to her simply because from time to time she needs to root herself in memories from a life before him, she used to think that night had pockets in which it carried and comforted and protected the poets of the world. A thought that now disavows all others, albeit not for very long. The night, this very same vessel of embarrassment, some years ago, when they traveled together, for no memory of him can be contained, when they traveled to a destination outside the edges of the map, though it was just that they had brought the wrong map, in winter, during a white night, this memory: her voice almost absent, his hands almost cold. A truth in its own right. This memory: at night, a knock on a door that perhaps was blue, or red, or green; the green from his paintings, not the green of forests but the green of all life; a knock, and then another; hours lost by the side of the road. Nothing, really, if one ponders upon it, just that it happened.

If I were to turn now, she thinks, and again we see her walking, If I were to turn, would I find, would I discover suddenly, surprisingly, absent from one step and present in the other, would I know how to locate the self without losing the present? Is there to be no continuity?

She thinks of this, and yet she does not turn; she thinks it as if outside of herself, unrelated to what her memories were flooding the body with just seconds ago; yet it does not come as a surprise, this thought, since it is, after all, a poignant relic of their life together: that she always thought what he had taught her to think, not out of submission, not even out of fascination with his mind, though such a fascination existed quite beyond any others; but just to travel these paths, not to allow them to be erased without her knowing how they feel to the touch, how they taste on the tongue. He taught her that to find oneself, to seek for what is absent, meant to lose what one already is. A transcendental task, to keep this lesson at bay.

A relic for him as well, a relic from his boyhood years, and from later, when he lost what he had already become, when first contemplating the discord of adulthood as it unraveled before him, when being struck by the indissoluble contradiction that no life is continuity enough.

If she were to return to the site of the grave now, if she were to pull her hand from the glove and brush away the snow. But no. She does not stop and she does not turn her head. In fact, she does not think anymore, except of poets and how they trample on with their little feet inside the pockets of the night; how there—there and only there— embraced by a comforting darkness, they have room to move, and find themselves, and move again, without losing a single fragment of whom they already were, of whom they have always been. Even what was closed to her understanding came alive there.

Inside the night, she thought, inside the night there is abundant space to place all selves.

Her selves, at night, one atop another, mingled togeth-er or exiled to corners, for there are endless corners and there are endless selves, and nothing but the night is able to contain them. Her selves, which, if she could hold now, if she could gather in an embrace and consequently be made aware of her hold over them—she does not know whether she would do so, she does not know what capacity she has, what strength to carry and care for these selves, and why would she even venture; she does not know why anyone would, why anyone would make space, in the night or anywhere, for selves already lost, for selves long-dead, for the manifestation of something that, to her mind, was more limiting than freeing.

Still, she thinks of them, she feels obligated to do so, if only to make sure no remnant of those selves can endanger her work, the creation of a *body of work*, a living body. She thinks and pretends to care for her old selves as to know, as to trick what remains of them, if anything, into revealing how they might tangle themselves with her present. In this, she sees possibilities of making and doing, possibilities of life on the outside of the heart, possibilities of miraculous creation and, even though she did not admit this, of an aberrant formalism, an adherence to a tamper-proof perception of what she must accomplish.

And whenever she does this, whenever her mind wanders, whenever she takes on this role, of witness, of lover, of caregiver; whenever she puts on this mask, no, this face, of salvation and anguish and perhaps mystery, for there remains, even in these lives she herself has lived, there remains mystery, and there are whole hours and weeks and months that she could not speak of—works of art, forgettings stitched on the heart—but whenever she goes through this exercise in leading what is left of her away from what she is to become, she feels as if the undoing is final. In her reading of this, in the case of this sickness, which is what she calls it, when impatient, when fed up, she fails to make the distinction between self as memory and self as real past, between the one that was and the one that remembers having been. Between the proper use of language and the proper use of flesh, albeit the flesh of other selves.

All is language, after all, she says to herself, whenever she might come close to understanding, whenever she might stumble upon differences that make the mind see, if only for a moment, beyond the trap it has set for itself. All is language and all is silence.

A gust of wind and her thoughts return to poets and how they slither like serpents through paradisiacal gardens; through the mind, through the air, through the cemetery, through the tunnel; disturbing the blanket of ice, disturbing sheets and fabric and pages deemed unworthy of being bound together, pages lying on the floor as if remnants of flesh from when one carved the ideal body. The *body of work* and the body of the beloved.

But she thinks of poets without truly knowing who these poets are, these poets who pierce the heart of the night with their gait. She thinks of them, these poets, without making out a distinguishable mark, and soon the words will jumble inside her head — her unuttered words will crash together bone and thought, skin and memory, hand and hair, scar and snow.

Poets devour all beginnings. She manages this last thought before all is confusion, realizing then in this sliver of a second that the voice of a poet is what she needs, that the voice of a poet is the voice she has been seeking, the voice to utter the words she has written; and while she thinks this, she allows the mind to travel other paths, as not to injure the tale, because now, when coherent, through coherence inside a chaos of its own, she knows that the tale is in need of a beginning, in need of fleetingness and beauty and instruments of torture, in need of unknowing voices and warm bodies. In need of two bodies that will hold it together until the narrator comes and describes it as she herself has planned it. Perhaps even in need of an aesthetic consciousness, though for that—for that and for that alone—snow, the most beautiful of characters, falls from the sky in pleats and performances; it falls to define, to distinguish; it falls to provide a trail so that the *body of work* can encounter the world. To receive this snow: what inconceivable pleasure.

After all, it matters not what words say, perhaps it never did; it matters not how words lay their claim; perhaps it always felt, to her but also to him, the lonely ones, that it was not for them to find this meaning that words are said to carry, and so now, in the narrow room, below her lines, he writes: Antinomies are only reconciled through rupture, through separation, only where the self becomes simultaneously the object and the subject that blurs all lines between the word and its own absence, between limit and possibility, between silence and synesthetic reverberation.

He writes, but she does not read. She feels separated from this. She, the invented one, the mirror of the other, of her other self, she feels herself disengaging but does not know how to wonder why. To this, he attaches no importance.

Outside their window runs the Seine, under the Mirabeau Bridge and everywhere run waters that once were, waters that have since returned to the place of their birth, to the core of this universe that she has created, waters from which she has pulled his body; waters that, having touched him, having known, having marked the flesh and reinvented the meaning of all symbols, come together and act now the role of a liquid déjà-rêvé, something recognizable to serve as background noise for the public phone that rings in the middle of the night, as contrasting color for shadows that move chaotically on the walls of the city, as measure and effort of time for these shadows without bodies, for how else would they know the direction in which to lean? How else would these shadows without the possibility of corporeality and forgiveness and transfer—how else would they find asymmetrical ways and temporal implications and instances of otherness?

And it is through these fabricated temporal implications that she herself finds enough meaning as to convince the mind and the hand that she must chronicle whatever it is that resides outside of their window, as well; it is by virtue of these waters that she decides the narrow room is not enough, by virtue of these waters that she says, I must flesh out in words and line breaks meant to one day piece back together this unresolved mourning, I must name these trembling rivers, these samples of fragmented existence and life outside the mind.

It is now terribly cold and the red of city lights all but removes any sign of what they are meant to be. This world, the real world, the one that relies on the reinvention of another, this world that breathes on the verge of death, this world lets out a final sigh and through it spins itself into the threads of rags long-abandoned. Inside the room, an exercise in narcissism, a text on the skin of the Other, a text about the self, a text placed there by the very understanding of these rituals, by this extraordinarily bountiful frame. Compulsion and movement take to the stage.

He plunges his hands in ink and traces the contours of her reinvented body.

They are both new, and this is the first night, the first necessary step, the passage that will unravel all passages, the collapse into existence, the night when, through the invasion of writing, on the floor, on the walls, and all along their bodies, they will learn, they will relearn—a splendid cinematic image: two amnesiacs, two beings rising from a carnal void, rising one on the body of the other. An ontology is in place. One day, having learned, he will listen out for wolves by putting his ear to her flesh and will hear the slippage of time.

And now..., she writes, pulling on a thread of letters that linger in the air, letters hesitant to position themselves; she writes to interrupt, to tame his eagerness, and so there is no need for the writing to go on, there is nothing she could add that would give them more than what two small words have given them: the possibility of breath. Breath as symbol and breath as what sustains the body. The continuity of memory. Their bodies: two dialects of the same language, two readings of the same page. She writes, and breath invades the room. She writes, and from this writing flows a metaphysical likeness that can have no other origin but that of ink.

Her ink in his brain.

The rise and fall of her breath, as they pause, as his head lays on her lap, as the hand writes without truly being controlled by the body, as anxiety lifts and language changes direction and falls heavy upon the room. This breath, hers, his, this shared breath — nothingness and outflowing and context to life.

The limit of this narrow space is but a threshold, and the hand knows how to make of the Other a thing to be known, how to make of the body an instrument of knowledge, and through it, through the choreography of this instrument, and through this knowledge, the hand knows how to discover the whole of the world. The world, at his fingertips. His fingertips, stained by ink and chalk and ruptures of space and time.

What follows therefrom reveals a completion that might be best explained by the image of a fire burning so tall and so bright that no extinction can reach it. Language stands at the foundation of this fire, and when there is no more language, when the letters are gone, when it is over, when uneasiness settles, for a moment, they bathe, they dress, they see the sea and feel the wind, they travel and sacrifice the flesh on this altar, of knowledge, of self-knowledge, for they must learn, and learn they shall. For a moment, he paints the waves. For a moment, she summons time as he once knew it.

He makes of himself an offering; she empties herself to receive it.

And through this emptying, she herself becomes the altar; she becomes the pretense and the text; she becomes love, and instinctual drive; she becomes communion and field of vision.

She becomes the very marrow of his bones.

To write like this, to write through the fervor of the senses, to write with an inclination toward erasure, to write with a language that is not language but the transformation of character into being; to write through the sexual act as togetherness, for they know of no other definition, they know of no other way to explain, to describe this touch, this perfection that they have found here, in the highs and depths of a room much too narrow to provide anything other than a beginning—a beginning for these two invented humans, these humans who nevertheless breathe, and touch, and offer, from not one but two abysses, they offer their newly formed minds to the trajectory of their hands; they offer it to the lust of their eyes, an instinct that follows no rule, that lives through them and them alone, an instinct that, when they were made to resemble others, their creator did not anticipate.

She did not foresee that they will want each other with other eyes, that they will touch each other with other hands; and yet, their eyes, their hands, their whole bodies, in this light, at this time, in this narrow room, if one were to look at them, if one were to study them with great care and attention, one would find that they are the eyes and the hands and the bodies of once-real people.

To write like this, to summon writing through this now timeless existence, at this instance, to have the whole of time, to give the whole of the self, to take distance and fragmentation and make them into flesh, to desire and pursue and exhaust and recompose, with skin anew and pores reopened: what inconceivable pleasure.

The invitation bestowed upon them, as they grapple with their newness, the repetitive nature of touch and discovery and momentum that grows and grows, everything subject to repetition, to compulsion, perpetually this invitation becomes for her the means to cope with absence, it becomes something with which to brush off the indifference of the wintriest of hearts.

It was in this invitation that she found a moment of actuality. It was in this that she recognized the present as something other than conviction, as more than the illusion of being which she had drawn repeatedly on paper and floors and walls; the present, not as metaphysics, not as florilegia, not as forever, not as hallelujah, but as mark on the real body.

And this is how she knows not to look in the mirror, through this she knows that she must not gaze at her body. Space and time and wound and decay continue to divide and separate, but she does not look, and so there is nothing there: nothing on the body, nothing under the snow. There is nothing but light, a light too bright for anyone to see beyond its vastness.

A light falling from the deepest darkness, as if it had no right, as if it were not real, and yet, a light nonetheless; a light that made of her heart a seal upon his heart, a seal that would ensure eternity. And it is in this, in this invitation, again, through this present and this presence, through this vision of the eternal, of the ordinary and the mundane, it is in this that she remembers the far-off emptiness, the nonworld, the trembling proximity of the void, the blue outside their window; repetition, and revival, and distance for miles.

This abundant use of language, this search amidst words and intentions and movement, this certitude at not knowing; not knowing who is speaking, not knowing who is writing, not knowing who is touching, not knowing whether language is written or spoken, remembered or forgotten. In this, through this, a fascinating passage: nothing on the tongue, nothing on the mind, nothing more but the will to say, Now or never, now and forever.

To illuminate it, this all-consuming attempt at freedom, this reading, a misreading, perhaps, scattered throughout the whole of the story; to shine upon it the light that shines now on their bodies, would be to travel to the edge of a world not yet developed, to fall and rise and gather in one's arms the secret signs left on the way by someone unknown, someone in revolt; a stranger, a promise, a face that never turns toward him.

To understand this, to make sense of these benign cries, of this enduring love, of these mountains and these seas and of the profound mystery of why—the why from earlier, the why from always—to walk the harrowing path of language that becomes less and less, of language in the service of meaning, meaning that diminishes, meaning that oppresses—language and meaning as artist and muse; to find otherness and call it need, to grasp desire and call it perversion—everything, any and all attempts are means of erasure, an erasure that once mastered, once performed, leaves the ground barren, an erasure that says: you have loved enough. An erasure that does not know how to escape itself.

And so there will be no illumination, there will be no understanding, and there will be no narrative thread, no exposure of the lover, no revealing of what marks it, no philosophical inclination toward anything at all, no exaltation of the soul at the sight of something firm and purposeful, no paradox of the carnal, no allegorical inter-pretation; there will be no reification, no distancing, no imprisonment, nothing but the hunger for true and perfect happiness, the hunger for exactly all that there is, how it is, how it will always be, now that there is eternity, now that the heart has sealed death outside itself.

It is as if without these words, without this fleshing, without this necessity, they could not embrace the eternal, even if they might keep on living in it, even if the com-munion remained. As if without these words, they would learn to ask for more than she could give them. And so she writes them. And from these words, he gathers a few of his own, which he then returns to her. A swarming mass of words; still wet, still undefined, proposed by her to him, by him to her, as means to a goal: the goal of learning, of relearning, how to write on each other's bodies, how to write and read and rely upon the skin.

And so, to last forever, for their bodies to unite and become this undying scattering of reality, they must spend hours and hours and whole lives writing, learning, reliving.

She must find the waters once more. He must yet again look up and paint upon the firmament his murals of blue. They must find the time before time and write it into their story, write with it their story; the story of two human beings: the lonely ones.

The limit of this narrow space is but a threshold. And so, they travel, and they find time, and with it, their story returns upon the page, their story fills the floor and walls of the room, and even if no one were to read it, in writing it—in writing it with the very flesh and ink of time—they made it so that it can last evermore. And thus the conflict remains. Now or never, now and forever.

Having written, they rest.

In the distance, to repeat a point perhaps yet unmade, in a place of lost unions, where ruins from other times give themselves to the wind, where rain falls and, in doing so, washes from everything and everywhere the very memory of itself, there, outside their window, or nowhere at all, an echo of everything already passed. The whole of time, manifesting itself like a deafening echo inside the shell of the present moment.

An echo that too erases itself, an echo that gives rise to a desire, and then another, and another, until the very end of all desires—in erasure, the satisfaction of something new, something bodily, animal; something that clutches and bites and tastes; something like a drive toward all things at once; toward oneness and otherness, toward oceans and rivers and water falling from the sky inside of rooms of feeble roofs, toward the courage to perform all actions and the apprehension to remember having done so.

In the distance, something renewed evermore through its very erasure. A writing. A coming together. A language. A culmination, not in the underworld, not in sleep, not in absence, but in this drinking of ink, one from the other; in this writing, of those who live, in the letters of those who in this very moment are taught that there are ways, that everything begins anew, in the words of those who write, for themselves and for their creator, who write that passing and remaining can be one and the same thing, as long as the mind teaches the body, as long as the body teaches the hand, as long as there is eternal passion, and malaise, and the essence of all experiences, bottled up, preserved; the whole of life, and consciousness, and touch, bottled up inside an inkpot from which to feed the existence of the only space that will have them.

SOMETIMES, in the space between them, he would whisper, If you were to die, if you were to find yourself motionless and breathless, if you were to close your eyes and go far away; every day, every night, small deaths, one after another, little deaths, regressions of states of consciousness, absorptions of life and air and all that keeps the body alive, your body, if you were to go farther than you have ever been, farther than you have ever imagined, then, but then and only then, think, know that the world too will disappear; that the world as effort, the world as impossibility, the world as pain will die with you. And that too is continuity, he would add, when the look on her face would tell him, would remind him that she seldomly thought of the world as for itself, nor of the world as for those who are inhabiting it. She very rarely thought of the world as anything but experience, as breadth of time and space and coherence, where bodies rest and minds lose track of themselves.

When she was ill, he would say these words to her; words that neither of them believed in; nevertheless, something beautiful and otherworldly; something menacing, even, at times; something threatening to alter their behaviors and views on life and how it passes, if ever they were to fall prey to its charms, to the charms of this little incantation, this little discourse on death and how it takes not the body from the world, but the world from the body, to fall prey to this thought: that a fragment, upon erasure, can bring about the erasure of the whole.

At night, in the darkness of the stage, a darkness comparable to resignation, at night, when what courses through the mind does so like time through the arteries of a world in chaos, this very world whose extinction they have contemplated now and then, here and there; yes, at night, when walking home enraptured by particularly dark impulses, impulses passing from one into the other, small electrical shocks to the body, when they touched, when their hands found one another, impulses subject to the same laws as the labyrinth, to the laws of spirals and nods and bifurcations and lines of communication; yes, at night, when it pleased him immensely to watch her think of such dilemmas. To be good. To be good in the world. To be good for the world. To be good.

At night, this narrative, this drive for life, this gaze seeking to redeem the whole of history in its waters.

This gaze, like the fullness of time.

At night, this double relation: gaze and what it falls upon. When to give oneself room for anything is to invite the darkest of darks, to commit the unforgivable crime of renouncing light; to become oneself a scene of tragedy and impulse and unreflective unconsciousness.

In the city, where their savage nature lay hidden in cupboards and between pages of books, where they might now relive their history, that was where he would say these words, that is how these words would come, above all others; a choice, a turn toward something soothing, an element of permanent significance, a reconciliation with physicality and all shapes of the world; a choice like a reconditioning of the mind. A choice like an echo—an echo of her need for structure, for the structure of a language invented, for the contingent realization of this invention. At night, when time beckoned them to explore further. To explore each other. When time beckoned him to slay darkness. When time beckoned her to burn her hands by dipping them into all fires. To make light; to become light. To burn and become light. For him. To release a flock of birds from within so that he could see them merge with trees and clouds and silhouettes and this image to paint upon her body. At night. When nothing is translucent, and nothing is known.

For a moment, in place of an intermission—for itself and in the world—from the darkness of such a night, from an existence trapezing between life and death, suspended not in time but in space, suspended high up where no one ever looks, where no one seeks for anything; a gentle coming; instrumental, like a sphere hanging by threads, emergent on the canvas of the sky, amidst trees and birds in flight; a coming like an intrusion that nonetheless no one takes notice of, an endowing of the self like a leaning against the earth, like a symptom of both separation and togetherness. For itself, and in the world, a coming, instrumental, like an adversity no phenomenology can account for and no human eye can perceive, for the simple fact that the body does not look and the mind does not think it. Something akin to the breaking of language into thought. Of thought into language. A coming instrumental for the order of the world, in this brief intermission, where there is nothing else but performance, no recognition and no empirical formation. Instrumental that there be such an orientation, such spheres resting outside of the human gaze, outside of the mind; that there be such acts of being, of waiting, of lingering, unperceived yet oh so meaningful. A project. Something to fill the hour, a twofold manifestation, the hour of an intermission, the hour of a time not yet defined.

As soon as the role of the story is resumed, as soon as it rebecomes, and as soon as it is again said that there must be positionings and through these positionings the visibility of past lives, in that very moment, like from the hand of a historian reconstituting from the evidence before him, an image takes shape, an image like a structure of language, an image like an invented memory. Two women on the green shore, a shore so green that it can only belong to a dream, a shore so outside of the real world, so discontinuous in its relation to the world, that one can only visit when rocked to sleep. Two women. A woman and her shadow. A woman and the bundle of memories she carries, placed to her left by someone, by anyone but her, for all she does is gaze toward the sea, all she wishes for is to escape it, this mass, this clump of have-beens residing beside her like a dark reflection; all she desires is to walk into the sea and find there other memories; memories of when she was asked questions for which she always had answers, memories of returning new questions, memories of an inside and an outside, an Eros and a Chronos, memories of a hand and its irreducibility.

And from this image, the memory of how they loved each other through questions and answers. How he found and offered tenderness in the asking of these questions, and sometimes, also in the answers she would provide, even when what she returned to him were other questions, even when, in every aspect and with every breath, she gave nothing but glimpses, indifference, a ceremonial indifference, something to become a memory; at night, in the darkroom, in the narrow room, in all rooms, this simple conjunction of vision and thought, floating freely amidst the objects of a reinvented world. Voice and wind and the inevitable structure of language.

There was much more: there were seasons and there were flowers of melancholy bursting from the chests of all new humans; there was grasping and gasping and the sensible presence of astonishment piercing the bone; there was life — through the body and in the mind; there were disappearances at the hand of nature and absences resurrected by the presence of words. There was the whole of blue inside a single day: winter by the sea. The sea, from which she emerged one night, gazing anywhere but at him. Him, standing there, waiting, on the shore, close to the waves she had troubled with her movement. There was obscurity, as she veiled her face with her hands when he began to speak of seeing. She wanted to hear it, this seeing, to hear it from his mouth, to hear the silences in between the words of this seeing, to measure breath and longing, and the fleetness of words on the tongue; she wanted to collapse the possibility of vision inside the echo of his voice, to gather there, inside that echo, everything the eye has captured thus far, and so she veiled her face with her hands. There was this veiling, and from under it, from under the curtain of fingers she would sometimes allow the mouth to speak, briefly, to speak and ask him why does time not suffice. There were questions and answers in abundance, and through them, they loved each other. It was as though the question itself was love, and the answer itself was love, and love itself was love and yet it had no bearing upon them, the invented ones, the recreated ones. There was all this, and they did not remember it, and so they loved each other with other eyes, they touched each other in the dissipation of other blues.

Just as he was about to utter something, as if knowing beforehand what he would say and wanting to interrupt his interruption, wanting to place before him the void of other words, of other ideas, of something that would contradict his own, she spoke and asked him about the need to fracture thought, about the need to speak of a sublime act, that of putting fractured thought back together. She would say, Why abandon oneself to stories that begin as all stories must, and not how they gush forth from within? Why to stories like all others and not to the story of all stories? She would ask this, like some kind of absolute conviction hiding inside of a question—a question that was not a question, but again, a positioning, of the body, of the mind, a taking into account of blood and the arithmetic of intimacy, for only in intimacy can one question—only in intimacy could she collapse like this, becoming one not with him, not with her belief, but with collapse itself. Only in intimacy. Only at the doors of the heart.

A reference, even, a reference to touch and sight and hearing, a reference to the existence of objects that one can come into contact with and to opinions that one can form; something to say, There are words, and existences, and senses, and there is something one calls mind, and from it, no abandonment can occur, no violence can come upon the reflexive self, no rejection can take the shape of a story, unless the story mandates it. Unless the story conditions: In the beginning was the Other.

She would say this and bury her face in her hands, she would say it and let cascading hair hide her moving lips; a decisive gesture, when naked, when consoled, when his arms would tighten around her and embodiment would become this ophthalmic substitute for essentially every-thing, which nonetheless could not be seen, nor could it itself see, but one knew — one knew that the shape of two embracing bodies, in nakedness, inside the metaphorical frame of a room much too narrow to be itself more than a metaphor, the shape was that of the roving eye; for long enough as to see without seeing, for long enough as to be-come relevant, contemporary; for long enough as to return to the oracle and ask with eyes and lips hidden, ask on what map can one find the home to where no return is ever pos-sible. A mass, a shape, a matter of responsiveness, of constructing construction itself, a matter of seeing, feeling, hearing the pulse of the body; a matter of being and opening, like the roving eye, putting itself in danger with every opening of the eyelids; a matter of two bodies, embraced. Consolation, in black, on the paper of a map like an answer to a riddle. A movement without end—sometimes alienation, other times the dialectical imperative of a union of profound consequence. Consolation, like prefix, like suffix, and everything in between. Consolation like the sexual act; consolation opening itself beyond itself, beyond them, beyond the world. Consolation like spontaneous combustion. Consolation, and they were one.

In providing this framework, she hoped to have led him to change the relativity of what he himself called senses, the relativity that he created for himself as explanation, as something emerging from the moments when he began to no longer see the world, the proper world, the world unraveling before him, when he began to no longer feel the specificity of these senses, to no longer measure as he once measured.

Amid invented objects and contingencies and precision and all such necessary contradictions, his body, out of consciousness yet still grasping for everything, for anything; for atoms and colors and the underside of things. What then was his body?

But consider now this textual embrace, for that is how she appeared to him when she was speaking, like text, like pages opening before him, with letters and punctuation in each pore; text that he would bring to his mouth and taste; bittersweet text, tender but alien, foreign and cold and scattered, and, at times, mere decorum that appeared out of nowhere as if it had always been there — as if she had always been there, placed by someone, not by him, for he does not remember when the always might have begun, and even if he could trace it, the memory of this always, he would find nothing in it but bare hands and shores too green to be real.

This image before him, that is how she now pictures it herself, when the forest burns steps away from her, this image aimed at the once-was, recognized only by the mind; now, when there is no sea, when no water flows to quench the thirst of this fire, of this grief, when there is nothing but a wrenching of the self, a wrenching away from the self. And what is it that he does, in this memory? She learns from this, from asking herself this question, she learns of a possibility: the possibility of remembering other lives, other paths, other hours spent in narrow rooms; other hours and other touches, any but the real one, anything but the coherence that should have been, the coherence of a life once lived, of a life that was supposed to provide enough answers for the tales to be spun, enough answers for the reinvention to be made possible.

Whoever identifies with him—and this is how she also learns of the problem, this is how she acknowledges that there is no one to identify himself with, no momentum to go through, that it goes beyond this and any alternative; it goes beyond rebirth and reinvention. She cannot abide by this malfunction.

There remains, however, this textual embrace, hers, an embrace that leads not to a narrative, nor to a character, not even—and this she knew all-too-well, how could she not—to a pleasant afternoon in the company of something he might recognize from all those other lives in which she had written him so many times before. The attempts, the mistrials, the fires. More fire. Other fires. Fire from above. Fire from all sides. Fire as sight and veil; fire as echo and mouth. Fire as the great refusal.

This is where you are now. A whisper directed to the empty room, as if to take ownership of absence, but also of the Other. This is how you are: a part of time, the part that travels, the part that stomps and tramples and places one foot, one heavy foot in front of the other, the part that shatters and is shattered, the part convinced that no harm can come to hearts like cobblestones. Everything happens here, where you are.

A perpetual object, this happening in the mind, so sublime and so enriching; a mode of being; reflective and wholly and in flagrant contradiction with the body. Everything happens there, and she must be able to remember it. She will remember it. She will remember movement as real intention and hand as real flesh. Nothing synthetic, nothing purely contemplative, nothing that might announce a forever without relief, a forever like a desecration of what she has so dearly crafted into becoming. Into being. This, she calls *love*.

In the sickroom, anguish and despair linger like traces of a beyond, they linger as if they too were real faces, belonging to real humans, as if they too were figures leaning against the door, figures partly transparent, figures confronted with the inevitability of death, of loneliness to come; figures destined to suffer by virtue of their names alone: despair and anguish. Figures converging toward the vanishing point of a future bearing no resemblance to the future held in prayer; no resemblance to the future invoked when one prays, or wishes, or simply makes for oneself in the mind a world free of exhaustion, a world where no sickroom exists and no orange-colored floor struggles to hold the weight of people passing through.

She has always thought of these rooms not as rooms but as some kind of thresholds; disaster-prone thresholds, points of connection between a world and another; not waiting rooms, something more ravaging, something eternal, doomed outside of its eternality. When it came that they had to prepare one for him, to build it from the absence of all things, he would joke — for how else could a sickroom have orange-colored floors and forest green walls and pictures hanging anywhere but where they should — but she does not remember, and by then, she was already absent from any and all rooms. By then, she felt herself flattened to the floor, she felt herself becoming not the image of pallor, but the orange shade he so desperately needed, for comfort, for invoking the skies of his cathedrals, for distraction alone. She felt herself disappearing and reappearing within a language of tragedy; she felt herself a garment of mourning, a long shawl, the longest; as if someone were using her to surround themselves with the already-formed screams of a death that had not yet come; a shawl wrapped endlessly around the throat of someone in mourning. A death like an intuition. A death like a many-voiced invitation. A death like a crime of treason against the compassion of all rooms. Born inside the diaphragm, a death like a river flowing without return. And yet a death no longer a matter of terror. A death belonging to everyday language. A death like a reversal of itself.

There are many kinds of love. Love that is as ephemeral as the human body. Love like the splendor of everything human. There are loves that, when placed in their appro-

priate context—historical, cinematic, temporal, corporeal
—appear to be resembling one another. They appear to
have become one the articulation of the other. Loves that
read like possibilities, like commitments to the flesh; loves
like drugs, like the process of purification, loves like ulti-
mate aims and loves like the intertextual dimensions of
the journey itself. Loves like corpses and loves that well
up inside the soul. There are loves that shine with such
intensity that everything becomes atemporal. Loves like
solitudes and wraths and everywhere, and in everything,
loves to the point of poetry. Loves beyond poetry. Loves
like silences from which distance is absent. There are many
kinds of love.

There are faces and heads and arms and legs; there is
logic, and proportion, there are crossings and theatrics;
there are desires and fantasies of form. Growth and flowing
and the cutting of flowers not yet prepared to be separated
from the earth that held them. All kinds of love. Loves
alive from the very beginning and loves never to exist in
the world. There are loves like missed encounters, forever
lingering inside the mind, and loves like temporalities akin
to cuts upon the body. Loves that fill the gaps in memory.

Loves that plague creation and loves that heal it. Loves
that are possible and loves whose impossibility is as necessary as the air one breathes. Loves like refusals and loves
that open on the verge of death. Loves like small abodes
upon the skin, inside the mind, around the body. Loves

like ruin, and chance, and negation. Loves responsible for the existence of the Other. Loves that can only become literature.

There are many kinds of love, and the eye does not know how to keep itself from wandering in search of such loves; in search of them all, every single one; these loves, their duplicates, their pulsations, their cores, their repetitions, their mirrorings; the thrownness and falling of these loves; in the world and outside of it; the eye wants all of these loves, it wants to become hole and fill itself with the liquid warmth of all these loves. And that too is paradise.

What does it mean to enter into the farthest depths of darkness? To inhabit it, to become its snaky head? Again she thinks of the night. Again she restricts herself to this thought alone. And in doing so, in realizing this thought, she senses the presence of time like something new, like something she has never felt before—time as it lingers next to her, time that lays its head in her lap, time that puts its arms around her, and retracts them, and then does so again; time like hesitation, time like love unrealized; time that injures and time that protects, time that adores and time that loves but does not say it; time that does not come and say: it is a dead man that you are punishing; time as it came on the stage, with its insides torn apart, time with its outstretched arms covering her body full of writing, in passing and throughout eternity; time that seeks refuge in the pockets of the night. She thinks of the night. Of being delivered over and over to this night. And here, in this thought, in this night, here is time, the very negation that confirms her existence; time, the infinite reference; time, limited by nothing but thought. Time as metaphysical desire.

What does it mean to wish time away? What does it mean to want to get rid of time that has nonetheless passed? Of time already produced, consumed, of time that no longer flows directly through the veins but time that has taken refuge inside the mind, of time that can no longer be erased for it erased itself and, in these invisible traces that it left, there will always be writing, and reading, and remembering?

Independent of such queries, she sets out to erase the minds of those she has invented—she sets out to erase everything she never gave them, everything she herself has forgotten. Yet her presence is not that of a character in a novel, and such designation does not even provide much meaning, not in the now, not in the conditionings of time as they sense it; time as embodiment of the eternal, time as the stillness of a page carried by the wind to other characters, other lives; a page carried well into the future, when there are chestnut trees and immortal flowers, and death comes as dialectical fulfillment outside contestation. When death comes and the arms are alive enough to open and receive it: a collapsing of the self into herself.

Human nature. A thought she immediately abhors, these words that sometimes cross her mind; these words like stubborn determinations, she loathes that they happen to come so, to come now, to come when there are cravings and climaxes, now when she must find ways, for there are ways; there are negations and approvals and circumstances under which all will soon be marked as possibility, all that has already happened. That is all she can say. That is all she can think. Human nature. Infinite distance. She abhors the fragility of this distance.

With no linear thread to follow, with nothing to support her, with nothing to guide her, she has lost sight, she no longer remembers the blue outside the window, the blue within the heart; she no longer remembers the sacrificial altar, nor the drawing or the writing, and for that matter, neither does she remember the past along with it. Her being-for-the-Other, she has lost all sense of it, and in her concrete reality, in her openness to rupture, in what materialized before her by virtue of this forgetting, there is but one joy: that there are paintings and structures and impossibilities which nevertheless resolve themselves, and that all of this is epistemology, that everything is epistemology. Enough so that she can replace, that from it she can rebuild, she will rebuild, she will rewrite and recreate and make from it an affirmation of two humans, of their reality, an affirmation like liquid consciousness upon the canvas of a night that falls for there is nothing else for night to do.

Behind the blue, behind the spruces, behind the ground like a frozen lake, no, above, necessarily above them all, a tiny red house, a white-roofed house, with windows so small that one might find it difficult to breathe; just the thought, just imagining these windows makes it difficult to breathe, for one is on the outside, always on the outside, and so there is no real knowledge, no epistemological motif, there is no real representation as to how large these windows truly are, and more so, there is no knowledge of how light might fall on the bodies inhabiting it, this house, no understanding of whether there are bodies, no reception of the fact that there are houses that even though look ordinary are anything but.

Salvation comes from the fact that one does not need to understand these windows, these evidences of multiplicity and presence of bodies within. Salvation comes from the fact that understanding is not required, and that, after all, understanding is not philosophy, and even if it were to be, there is no need for such insinuations, inasmuch as they belong to the realm of the dismembered, to the land of disfigurement, and to death that holds no measure of grace. They belong to the space of horrible, indescribable mutilations upon the page, where one thinks and writes and in that lettering one places, artificially, an understanding of the world as world, of the house as house, of the body as decaying flesh.

But there is running water, there are rites, and rivers in which the body can bathe, there are returns and under-goings, there are possibilities and there are walls to lean on and words to write. Other words, words that are gentle, words that are kind, words that speak of the Other, words that survive, words that hold significance beyond their limiting definitions, words like great civilizations of the past, words like anything sheltered and loved and kept forever in existence. There are words. Half-glimpsed. At the mercy of chance. Words, hauntingly, everywhere. Words like them, in the narrow room, two humans, the lonely ones.

Behind the blue, there are red houses like lovers motion-less in the swaying embrace of time, isolated, unfathomable; red houses like the fruits of a forthcoming, red houses like hearts pulsating back to life, red houses like occasions and proofs and absolute truths.

A tiny red house, someone once remarked, Just a house.

A house like a massacre. A house like a rupture in the canvas.

A beautiful echoing, this memory, a criterion now for assembling all that she has gone to assemble; a house, amidst spruces; a house he made for her; a house on the beach; a house, emergent, on the highest of crests, in the deepest of caves, a house from the hands of a painter, from the mind of a writer, from a beautiful creator of tiny red houses.

She is able to apprehend the nature of this red house. And that is happiness. That too is paradise. She is able to situate this house inside the human space of the mind. She is able to create correlation and contain absence and presence and coming-into-being inside of its redness. She is able to carry this house.

She thinks of the house and she thinks of nightfall, and through these thoughts no thread passes, nothing to hold them together, nothing to untie solely so that there is something to tie back together, no framework, no illumination from her to him, no relation to the self as self, nothing to hold onto as one steps into the coming time, no thread to capture the torment of the present, and no thread to bring about the infection of the body. Nothing to ask: Who are they? Nothing to brush up against her body, or his, against the body of time. Nothing to hold the hand when it aches no more, when it is frozen and snow falls. There is however, a kind of totality, a root, a mark, a contribution, something that makes her travel to the end of the world, for no other journey is befitting. No other journey can gain the role of a character and act like a contradiction upon the senses. No other, but the path toward the place where no path begins. And there — she finds there a tiny red house, like a massacre on the canvas.

And yet, however bleak, however dark, however present, this lack, this haze, this confusion, this prosaic confusion, its memory remains, and through it, she can compose, she can escape, she can accomplish, and she can do it all away from the cruelty of prying eyes. And this too is paradise. However bleak, however dark, however appalling and even vicious to depict, to follow this, nothing but the realization of a chapter about succumbing to the madness within, a chapter about serpents and sinfulness, such dreadful notion, concept—pyre and battlefield and formal consecration— a chapter about primordial separation, a chapter without which she could not have said, Come, and then go on forgetting the existence of the one she was summoning.

This chapter, in itself not complete, is like a shudder through the body that, when encountering a cold wave, does not know what to make of its touch and all it can do is give way for the eyes to take in the presence of water. A shudder through a body that never learned to close its eyes when water comes and it drowns the senses.

A chapter without which no descent into chaos would have ever been permitted by nature. A flushed chapter, breathing heavily, a flow of blood under the skin, through neighboring veins and the immensity of flesh as keeper of words. A chapter in the state of being written. In the state of being read. A chapter. A hidden substratum; subtext and the disintegration of the self, all in this very chapter, inorganic matter on the floor, in a dark corner of the room, inorganic and not much to the touch, inorganic and nothing to the taste. A chapter ensuring continuity. And this too is paradise.

The stage changes and once more there are lights. There are lights, and there is nothing one could lose in gazing at their brightness. Nothing one could lose in seeing time, with armfuls of desolation and sadness and silence—most of it silence—time chased away by laughter in the street, time forced into hiding by joyful and ecstatic disorders.

Nothing one can lose by gazing at these disorders, these conditions, one by one, like concrete, historical events, like transcending presences and real existences: to be human, to be infatuated with the impossible, to be moved, to want to drink from the sky and from the sea and from deep within the well of eternal life.

The stage changes, and here is time, the poet, creating darkness: the poem. And that too is paradise.

IT COMES NOW THAT SOLITUDE..., but she must have dreamed it, for there is no continuance to this thought, this too a solitude in itself, marked by the abandonment of something not yet whole; this phrase unfinished, the unuttered thought; and there is no pleasure in seeking one, no pleasure in drawing out the matters of lacking language; no pleasure in completion but for when the flesh seeks it, again, solitude in itself; and so she abandons herself to her steps, as she walks, still; as snow falls, still; she abandons herself and goes farther and farther from the grave, through paths of foam, through reclaimed shapes and grass and meadows; yes, whole meadows at her feet, meadows like shores, meadows like ledges; through an abyss that darkens and through worlds that are ending; ahead of him, from other years, ahead of his thoughts like clusters all around the skull. If they were to disappear, in this very moment, to disappear from all hours, from all days, from all years and from the whole of existence, if this solitude were to grow, and grow; if this silence were to fall, and fall—perhaps this could fix her heart for a while. For as long as the dis-appearing act lasts. For as long as the curtain allows it.

A frame of absorption, of formation, something like the cinematic process: this consolation, his words as he offers them to her; his voice as she receives them. And yet, the constant fluctuation between the meaning of these words and the warmth they induce is something that is denied to him, that is, if she were to say them, if she were to speak to him about how when he will die the whole of the world will die with him; if she were to put before him this clear image, the same that he turns to in order to com-fort her, it would result in nothing but a progressive dark-ening of the mind. It would rupture between them and place there an insurmountable distance. He does not wish to hear it. This death, long talked about, he does not wish to hear of it any longer.

If they were to disappear. An unflawed resolution. Phantasmatically. Barely visible and then not at all. Nothing but the preprimed canvas. A convalescence of the wander-ing eye. Charcoal and oil and lithographic chalk, erasing themselves slowly from the canvas of the world. Solitude. If they were to disappear, what then would fill the space in between?

There are days when his vision is disturbed to the point of no longer being able to read. Days when he lingers by the window, holding his head in his hands, gazing in the distance at nothing at all. Days when the blue lies not outside but within. Days of laying bare that which was hidden by the possibility of sight. Days when he distances himself from everything and anyone, at the far end of a room so narrow that to reach the window from the door one needs only to put together a thought, and then another, and there one is, by the window, gazing at nothing at all. Days when he lingers there, in silence, saying to himself, If there is something, beyond the eye, beyond the gaze, something to transcribe what the hand feels, something to depict how the moment comes and allows itself to be touched and not gazed upon, if there is something, it is not out there, in the street. And yet, that is where he lingers, his back turned toward her, toward the room, toward his words on the floor.

There are days when the memory of time is but a fragmentation on the skin, when time comes as a black spot on the eye, as conversation with darkness. Each and every one of these days, set apart one from the other, by something small, by something trivial, by something out of sight; a rite, a measure, a pronunciation. Days when there is no finitude, for the eye cannot grasp it. During these days, when everything lies beyond the reach of the ordinary, she spends her time reading to him. She reads to him, sometimes in silence, oftentimes in silence, so that only the act of reading can be heard: pages, fingers, a gasp now and then. Circulating, lingering in the echo of these sounds, under the sign of this act: to read to him; to read to him when there is no strength in himself, to read to him when what he wishes to write or to paint or simply to gaze at has no means of expressing itself. The narrow room becomes then a darkroom. It becomes a lecture room. And in it, through the reception of this act, like an implicit presence: silence. Silence as the primal form of intimacy. Silence as the first elegy. Silence as the possibility of all languages. Silence, bearer of vision. From this silence, from her gestures, the eye recaptures its sight.

In her hand, a small note: All will be well.

It breathes, the writing on this note, it breathes by itself as if it were a living being; the rise and fall of these letters, their indentations, that is how they feel to the touch, when she holds and crumbles it in her hand, as breaths upon the paper, as breaths in the grove of her skin; these letters, endowed with a consciousness of their own, with a personal consciousness that no uttering would be able to reproduce. Yet she utters it nonetheless. All will be well. And in this, through this voice on the margins of existence, in this there is an element of blame, of guilt, a more-than-human element of fault that seeps into and from the brain. A falling into the embedded ways of memory, when memory comes and it represents a viewing that goes beyond the self, when it comes not as memory of the past that she has lived but as memory of the past that was embedded on the skin, as memory of another life, the public life, the life delivered to and from the darkness of others; and in it, this blame, when reading his note, when remembering not what was, but how it was seen. A glorious means to subjugate, through one's very voice, through one's very memories. Shipwrecked, the voice utters again. All will be well.

He reaches his hand in his pocket and finds a small projector there. It is spring, and every now and then, when they pause for a sip of water or the gesture of smoking, the gesture of something they used to do, a gesture like a pressing of lips into language, a permeability; this gesture, the only drug they are abusing; when she looks down and fidgets with the unlit cigarette, then, he removes the object from his pocket and mimics the movements of someone who is about to project a film on the wall of whatever building lies before him. Movements she had never before encountered. Movements she would have never known, if it would not have been for the fact that he decided, early on, to do this for her, for them, when pausing, when lingering. Anywhere, everywhere, this catharsis.

It lives in the mind, stitched upon its surface, this action, the representation of this action; the tradition, the motif when no motifs are needed; it lives on the surface of the mind that they have created for one another, a mind, a gift, like two brains, conjoined. It lives and breathes and that is how she now sees it, when closing her eyes, clear as waves lapping at her feet, clear as raindrops on the skin, even if her back is still turned, even if the darkness of the night allows for no sight at all, even if roots and skin and the sea, the sea itself; no, not skin, flesh, exposed, the flesh of time — time with its insides torn apart, time like an animal that comes and lingers at her feet, time wrapped around her in an embrace not even its passing can erase; time, her protector; and through the presence of time, she sees it, she sees his hands, a scar right below the left index finger, projecting memories into the night. She sees it, inaccessible and sublime.

She sees his hands and knows that the nonliving has existed before the living, she knows that these hands, pictorially, will soon be reduced to nothing but afterthought, and yet, look, how real, how identical to the real, beyond their very name, the role of these hands projecting film; these hands, like healing wounds, like wounds that heal; these hands, small embers on the body; manifestations and indentations and exceptions made of death; these hands, like withdrawals; these hands, in the left margin of a paragraph and everywhere at once; these hands, like essentiality and sex and brackets in the structure of thrownness; these hands that would touch, but alas, they cannot reach; these hands that would write, but alas, they no longer remember how; these hands, in the right margin; these hands, from nothing; these hands, to all things anew.

To return now to these hands, to have these hands be returned to her: what inconceivable pleasure.

The day before last, for there is a last day, and there is a day before it, and there will always be a day before, a day to walk the length of the cemetery, a day to name all streets, to utter all words, to gather all souvenirs; a symbolic day, a day to abandon, there and everywhere, not a body, not two, but all the bodies in the world; a day to cross rivers and enter tunnels, a day to do everything one must do, a day for preparation, a day to take the arms of time and twist them until there is no movement but that toward the past, until there is no text but the severed text, the fragment, the text that looks back on its rupture and smiles in the shape of an erasure; a day to twist the arms of time until there is no act but that of touching, when touching had not yet been invented, when no one had yet touched, when there was no first touch, and there was no touch before the first, and there was no hand that knew how to do anything but write; when there was no hand but the hand that writes. No hand but her hand.

And there is no story, there can be no story; neither myth nor tale, not when other stories align like untruths to fill the missing pieces, when other stories strive to write these lines; there is no story when grief runs through the veins, when grief holds the pain, when grief is paper itself; no presentation of such a story would be possible, and so that is when she grasps it, not in myth, but above her head, The sky might break open any minute; and in saying this, in this incantation, she knows that she might be replacing one death with the possibility of another, but never one love with the memory of another.

In doing so, in lashing out against this myth, against all myths, for to think and to say it is to erase it from the book of myths; to think it is to render it commonplace, an act of the day-to-day; it is to take from it its conscience and throw it far into whatever waters will have it now, soiled by the mundane, into whatever waters offer to clean it and gift it to other times, to other years. To make of it a testimony of falling. And in this she knows, there are times when desire flows and escapes and returns only through other territories. In this she knows, the altarpiece is another, time is another; but he, he must never be another.

Never having turned, she walks ahead, the cemetery far behind, farther than a minute ago, still allowing space for his thoughts to gather, space for the eye to wander along-side them, to wander and perceive and make from this a fabric, a fabric for itself, something, a veil behind which to hide. She leaves space to anything and everything, she leaves space, so that nothing comes to knock at the door of her mind, so that nothing can manifest itself as form and phenomenon, nothing, not even another kind of interpretation but for the one she already chose. She walks ahead. A moment in which they could both disappear, if disappearance were indeed what they desired, if she could, she, the determined; if he could, he, from other years; if they could abandon a world in the middle of breathing life into it. But it is not disappearance that either of them seek.

It is not to be robbed of meaning that they seek. They wish to bathe in all meaning, to become one with all that there is, at once; simultaneity through the senses, through the mind, through the body, through whatever pore will absorb it; to be star high above and rock upon the ocean floor and like this to meet, still; to be entire paragraphs and mere words. To be. To be the end of something just as something else is about to begin; to be something, enough of something as for no name to hold it; to be in all and through this all, through this everything, to be the measure of human existence; this beautiful measure, when lips quiver, when the hand stains the wall, with ink, with paint; when the hand climbs the ladder of writing; when the eye, benevolently, lets a veil fall upon its wanderings through the world.

They wish to be this logic of abandonment and the brutal essentiality of the wounded; to be the wound itself; to be healing and innate creation. To be, they wish to be, and give rise to unity and consequence and balance. To be disinterested spectators and that which will soon grip them. To be thorn and flower and the paths of all trains. To be the gusts of all winds; to be hour, and time, and passage; the beautiful, the ugly, the death of all prayers. They wish to be words that fail and words that salvage. To taste and devour each other and from this devouring to be born anew. To be in the margin, left and right. To be impending darkness and eternal return and red house. To be the tomb from which everything is reborn. To be the corpse that feeds life anew.

Everything. When they were alive together, when he was alive, when they were anxious and in love and connected one to the other and to the world, that is what they wished for: to be everything.

To be everything, and for that everything to have a conscience and for them to drink this conscience, and from it to rebecome, again, everything. All at once. Silence and the silent. The historic origin of the world. Primordiality and authorship and skin that never learned how to die.

She writes all this not on the floor, not on the blue walls of the narrow room, she writes it on a piece of glass, large enough that it could be a window, which she holds tightly against her chest; a pane of glass large enough to shelter entire phrases; tighter and tighter as she writes, burrowing into the skin; a glass large enough that if she wanted to, she would write there the whole of their history; if she wanted to, she could draw maps, and lines, and circles; deeper and deeper as more words come; tightly against her skin, so tight that blood mingles now with the ink, and this is when she stops, when enough words have become red as to draw her attention; she stops and dips her fingers, not in more ink, but in this blood, her blood; she dips her fingers and reddens her lips. A gesture out of consciousness; a gesture like a litany, cut off from life; a gesture that paints a massacre on the lips.

For all the nostalgia that she might feel, for all the impulses, and reasons, and functions she might feel obliged to honor, when her face is turned, not toward him, but toward the spectator who gazes at her, the spectator she has swiftly written on the glass, whose existence she has invited and invented on the spot, for someone needed to be there, someone needed to witness her oscillating between forgetting and remembering; between forgetting the lines of his face and remembering the taste of blood. Someone had to witness, as grotesque as it might have looked, the correlation, between the skin that is wounded and through this wound invites the mind to remember, and the mind that writes, and through this writing, invites the body to forget.

They wished to be everything. A fantasy, in her eyes, resting in the chambers of his heart, a question unanswered, a too-tight an embrace, a move toward an absolute like a sadomasochistic drive, an urge to have everything inside of them, to devour and then crave more; an urge to carry everything and share it between themselves and themselves alone, and swallow it whole before it can settle anywhere but there, in the space between, before it can properly become something that moves and lives and finds out that another world exists, before it can become something that separates itself from the mass in which it took its first breath, original truth before its origin.

This was thus their only resolution, their only belief, essentially amoral; an utterly condemnable world view; a burial, in perpetuity; no rest, no pause, an act of burying everything inside a self made of two people, like a grave made to contain what they themselves could not understand on their own. A collaboration, a literary and egoistical collaboration of mind and flesh, a coming. A coming together unto the ruin of creation.

On the floor, in the narrow room, where he rests, where all thoughts occur, this tiny fragment of impossibility, another impossibility: there is but one desire, the desire to cut the head of endlessness. Consumption of that which is without end.

In the darkest parts of the room, always as if under the floor, like a river flowing unnaturally, this wish, just below the visible line of what she allowed there; this river, alone in the world, an almost black desire: to consume that which is without end. To burn the endless forest. To gulp down the eternal sea.

He picks up a piece of chalk and wants to write about the scattering process that makes the sky blue, but all he can think of, all that his hand allows to manifest is how she once reached her arms so high up that, from afar, from where he was then standing, from where he had been watching her without disturbing, it looked as if she were a trapeze artist on a stage made of clouds and blue that went on for miles and miles. To wander the streets and fall in love with a trapeze artist. To stop and say to this stranger: I love you. A bygone stage.

She remained there, her arms high up, stroking the blue of lost horizons.

There is but one desire. A desire as cold as the body that once harbored it. Now, from this desire, nothing remains but metadiscourse on the floor of the room, without any indication as to how to destroy it; nothing but similarity with what once was; without any instructions as to how she can keep it as—as memory? as art and gap and possible ritual of mourning? As enigmatic statement about the shape of damned resistances and flowers that wither even though they are called immortelles, flowers that wither under the human condition of superiority and indifference and whatever onerous picture might one paint when thinking of how to end endlessness itself? But now, the human condition was not his condition, it was not his desire that was black, it was not his desire that spoke of something cruel and authorial and demanding, of someone in conflict with himself and with the world. Of a perversion. Of something that contradicted the very purpose of breath: to allow for one final day.

In order to grant himself this desire, in order to capture and retell, he must find ways to make a pleasure of memory. To make of regained selves something pleasurable, something he is able to house within, for enough time as to escape the crashing down of everything. In order to speak, in order to tell her, in order to learn how to speak and tell her of this desire, he must not confuse nor conflate the very existence of what he is asking for, of what he is wishing. His desire remains that which he must integrate into language, that which must be made real through utterance, through speech, through insistence and through the motions of the text—the text as dialogue, the text as narrative, the text as correspondence.

It must have been the beginning of summer, when everywhere, in every painting, in every text, outside of every window, one could grasp a relic of creation. Creation left from spring, albeit exhausted; creation, albeit a direct cause of suggestions and bones and displacements.

Creation—and in it, she came to understand, there resided a certain kind of closure, something to cry out from there and say that the season is false, that time is misguided, when it tightened its arms around her, when it protected her and told her through the gusts of the wind, All will be well. Summer, like a call to identity, no, a call to love the Other more than oneself. Summer, like a fluid name dripping down the body of all seasons. It must have been summer; they must have been in their first year together. All was well. Such are the errancies that traverse her mind when she tries to hear herself, to hear him, to hear the years as if there were broadcasted on the radio, the errancies she permitted, these small yet so significant incomprehensions, these moments that came to her, when alone, when writing, when drawing, when making sense of a correspondence that no longer was. In summer, when other summers came to her, memories of torrid nights dabbled in blue, and green, and the half-light of the city; memories of lingering so close to one another that no breath could pass anywhere but from the mouth of one into that of the other, so close that their lips were almost touching; nothing around them but the silhouette of a tree, or perhaps that of a street lamp, they couldn't tell, and even if they could, she would not remember it now, for the whole of everything was green, and severed, and it appeared just so that no memory could ever portray the details it concealed. It was summer then, and now, when time comes again to speak of the uncanny

—she does not know the season, nor does she make of it a question. Time has returned to speak of absences. To make all memories appear as if they were a single one. To make the mind a highway, a place of wandering in search of this one memory. Time came again as it always did, and said that there is no warmth and there is no amorality. That there is but one desire, and now, through his veins, runs the ink that will offer him not the realization of this desire, but the very contrasting substance that will reverse it.

On whatever page, on any and all pages, this tale, written as if a part of all tales, as if to leave something unsaid, as if to leave aside the disparity, as if to leave aside that they are fated to give themselves deafness and blindness and anything but what the other desires; that in closeness, in intimacy, that in his last year, when he wanted nothing else but to strike life with a single blow; in his last year, she took it upon herself to plot and plan and write down the specifics of something she did not even understand properly, not at the time.

The contrast and constrict of these two wishes, a mind on the verge of erasure, a mind slipping into unkindness, the nature of it, left aside from the telling of this tale, from its introduction and its end, unless one were to read it in too deep a silence, unless one were to find something there that speaks of it, in the blank space, unless one were to go looking behind the stage for this uncanny secret, her inhumanity, incorporated but not uttered. Left outside of time as she knows of it. Something that perhaps would have convinced her. Everything; as last wish, as single wish, as formation of the one and only coherent desire: to cut the head of endlessness, to no longer be; not as another, not as double, not as creation inside a narrow room. And yet—

There is but one desire.

ANOTHER NIGHT COMES. A recurring darkness. It snows and snows, and in this perpetuity, she feels that time can no longer be recognized, that time can no longer be seen and understood; there is no longer a corporeal constitution that allows for it, and she feels now as she looks: frail, battered by the passing of months; in this perpetuity, no unity other than that of the whiteness that falls from the sky, no continuation other than that of this substance that freezes disintegration itself. A metapoetic consequence. But no. Nothing could freeze this collapse, for in such a freezing, an end might come. A crisis of form. She smiles but does not speak. There is no one to speak with; there is nothing but ink spilling on the floor and the blurring of boundaries, and in this blurring, in this secret force of nature, in this erasure beyond the measures of erasure permitted to humans and creatures and objects that might have, for a single moment, possessed some kind of life inside of them; in this, underlined, evident: the unfamiliar, the sun that nevertheless rises over an unknown land, again and again; the laws of a city that never was; abjuring and renunciation, as she smiles still, far from being one and the same, far from being opposed, far from being a mechanism of biology, far from being anything at all, really, but something that one perhaps should not believe, something itself freed from belief.

A sight as if from the shores of imagination. A landscape, a realm, something, a glimmer of snow falling to the ground. Something that should not be, the ambivalence of both worlds, of life and death. The idea of being buried. The idea of breathing. Contrast and account and counterpart, limited, yet providing further evidence of what the snow has covered beneath her feet.

A remarkable time for life on the stage. For life in a museum. For life inside the painting. And in this painting, two humans, the lonely ones, embraced, with their backs toward any gaze that might fall upon them; embraced, toward the forest, heads leaning on each other, arms intersecting as if to rest one on top of the other. A remarkable time. A time that will never again let itself be recognized. A metaphor for what is to come. The spectacle of nature as a psychological landscape in which two humans can shelter themselves from the world. There are numerous versions of this nearness. Numerous variations of walking, embracing, toward the welcoming forest. The lonely ones. Lost. Two humans, accompanied one by the other. Placed together in isolation. There are variations in which only one of them can be seen, the other removed from the landscape, erased from the canvas, kept outside the gaze. Variations of white shimmering in the light, of hair waving in the wind. Variations of head in hands, facing the undulating shoreline. There are variations as paintings, as life on the stage and in museums; variations of life, as they have lived it, as they have gazed upon it; life as consideration, and reservation, and admission of faith. Life as physicality and grasp and passage from one into the other; life as thrust and moment and liquidness. For a long time, life as warmth and exposure; life as coexistence and primacy and romantic exigency. For an even longer time, life as voice, life as cobblestone, life as projection and mural. One has to wonder, one might wonder, why life like this, life like an organ in the body, life easily excisable, life discordant, life as pressure and indentation upon the surface of memory? Why life, thus, why life in blue and life as massacre and life as light that falls without there being a need for such a falling? Why life that is rewritten, readapted, restaged? Why language outside of itself, why touch outside of the body? Why life as a marching toward the forest and not the sea? Why life as a marching toward the sea and not the forest? Why life, brazenly, carnally; life arriving at the unattainable, life as nature and life as destruction? Why life that cuts through the narrative and removes all signs of plot, all traces of linearity? Why life, in its depths, becoming, rebecoming, life again? Why life, eternal, materialized on the skin and inside the heart; life, restless, generous? Why life as question and answer and the play of the wandering eye? Why life as an affirmation of death? Why life as thought, and in this thought, modesty and vertigo and the idealistic interpretations of all things? Why life, recreated, life as unkindness, life as the denial of desire; life as the return to an idea that fails to explain its own outcome? Why life as error and symbolic passage? Why life as sex and longing and the rupture of all things temporal? Why life as blue and jubilation? Why life as eroticism, as deviation, as hand upon the heart and rope around the thigh? Why life that is at grips with its own existence? Why life as fragment and the force of a return? One has to wonder: why life at all?

The falling snow now provides the impetus for all things. Snow that augments and snow that completes. Snow that illustrates and snow that inaugurates. Snow that falls and snow that fathoms and merges. Snow that is permitted to fall. A snow that undertakes to speak. Snow as conclusion, snow as natural law, snow as main protagonist. Snow as unreality. Snow as the movement of the mind manifesting before the eye. Snow as prophecy and snow as actual existence. It snows; it falls, but it is the fall of other years.

In the armchair, she reads something akin to imper-
manence, as her eyes pass from the book to the whole
of the room; she reads inattentively, her lips sometimes
uttering aloud the words that the eye encounters or the
names of objects from the room, other times as if placing
themselves on the ghost curves of an invisible neck. She
reads absentmindedly—absent not from herself, not from
her surroundings, but from the book itself, as to be able
to drop everything at the slightest sign, in order for the
book to remain thought and the body to remain capable
of movement. A theatrical testimony of the downfall to
come. Of the downfall already here. Of something, anything; something to urge, to come, and scream, and say
that there is life and this life is the inverted sea, that this
life is the beach, and the handwritten note on the table,
and the cutting of images in the darkroom. That there is
life and this life is climax and wave and moment in the text.

From the first page, the words and phrases suggest that
what is in fact visible is the metaphysics of the soul, in permanent communication with the borders and restrictions
that such a piece of writing might force before its readers.
From the very first page, this downward, this sliding into
something tentative, ambiguous, where no dialectical rela-
tionship between the senses exists.

An isolation she shakes her head at—the nonuniversal-
ity of this thought—inherited and excluded and altogether

much too normative, if she were to focus on its tragic implications, on the unresolve of these implications, on the suffocating effect that they produced; much too normative to
allow it a place, a plot, a thread in her world. A clarification
of sorts, something that she would no doubt be able to
provide, but no one asks, and so what she articulates is for
herself, and finds it exhausting and unneeded. There is no
conflict, and thus the mind pauses its attempt at creating
one. The page remains intentionally blank.

She reads. An assignment she accepted as a trial run.
It must have been some ten years ago. The first book they
gave her was a 1783 trilingual treatise on plants, a book
she kept more as idea in the mind than object in hand,
a two-lined gap, a fragmentary something, a white space;
a poem, even, all this only if she were to treat it just right,
as a narratologist would; if she were to read it, not as she
was instructed, but as the book itself wanted to be read.
For a first time, for no last time. If she were to open it and
gently touch its pages with her fingertips; an image, a film,
filtering from it anything related to the process of reading,
leaving nothing but the visual, the basis of all memories,
no longer concerned with any other parts of itself; the
slippage of time as the hand caresses the page and the
page comforts the mind. A treatise on plants. An exposition on the life of other readers, other writers, a literary
sublimation, renewed with each new opening, with each

whirlwind, with each brushing aside of kindness and suspicion and the absence of any other books. A treatise honoring her isolation, lashing out against the misinterpretation of early times; nothing but a treatise on plants: names and tables and images, faded just enough as to speak of anything else but the root and the stem; faded just enough as to become a manifestation of aesthetic possibilities.

During this time, in the course of these years, she made herself into a theory of the eternal reader. She, who in the end did not even know what a narratologist was. She, who did not know what made her one or when or what it was that she was doing now, with these books, why she read them; she, who otherwise pondered very little on her literary concerns. What was it that she was writing down in one notebook after another? She, who did not necessarily want or need to be one, to be indecision upon the lips, hesitation of the mouth agape; to be an image of this impossible profession, something she might one day make up for herself as to fill a gap. But she will not remember. She will only remember his brushstrokes, and so she'll say: Perhaps I was a painter.

She reads what they put before her, it has been so for many years, but she also reads what he writes, in the narrow room, pages on tenebrism and identifying with matter and with the experiences of the man who wanted nothing; notes on how he once saw the world in bright shades, when he knew all colors, when absent from it were all shades of violence and destruction and evil; before there was darkness, before there was art and theater that brought the idea of wastefulness to his feet—improvidence —notes on the emergency of death, on primordial orgies and forms of disintegration. Sometimes she is tired, and glosses over the details, over names of authors or mentions of cities, which he places amidst what she calls the chaotic beauty of these theories. Sometimes she is tired and she misses when, for instance, he writes about philosophical poets; she misses when he writes about Greek cities amidst depictions of childhood splendor, such as flower-brimming fields or forests without end; illuminations or seasons in hell. Analyses of light. Once, she missed him writing: Death is a threshold. Something which she herself believed, but in what they differed was the fact that what awaited over that threshold was not the same for both of them, and perhaps, knowing this, they might not have remained standing for so many years; perhaps, knowing it, remembering it, she might not have layered this new life as she did, she might not have written and whispered, Come. The dark undercurrent of these writings—she has forgotten enough of how she used to communicate with him and with the words themselves as to allow, as to wish, as to make possible a rebirth, and in this rebirth, to give them new meaning, new interpretations, new possibilities of correspondence.

When terribly tired, she even missed whatever traces

of her there were in his writing. Rushing over words that spoke of her, over pages that, from afar, from a proper distance—far enough that one might not even be able to read the words but rather just see them and recognize them as words—rushing, she began to see it all as a kind of ode to the human condition, same as what she would at times encounter in philosophical writings about words like *light* and *fire* and *time* and *desire*, when reading them, as if she were not in the narrow room, nor in the tunnel, nor cradled by furious waves, but on a park bench, contemplating, discussing the convulsions of annihilation and coincidence and limbs that reach for one another in dreams and words that are themselves too convoluted to count. A reasoning that tormented her.

The eternal idea of the wise person, she says to herself, forgoing it the moment she uttered it; as if she had found the perfect answer to something unrelated, something that had been troubling her for years, because yes, this is what had always bothered her about her readings, about the manner in which she was instructed to read. A thought she nonetheless brushes aside seconds after it comes to her.

An excellent moment. A moment of excellence. The fabric of the soul, unfolded like silk on the bed. Captive within, resting, the effort for postponing the end. And while she rests, it comes to her that this is not decomposition, that these days in too-swift a passing are not part of the manner in which the world decays, that these nights darkening their walls are not an integral part of time, that they will be returned to them, over and over, endlessly, infinitely; it comes to her that what rots and what lingers is in fact one and the same, and inside a story one can place lucidity and thought and so many other stories that the mind might find itself breaking open and rain might fall, as it often does, when there is a story, and someone who wishes to tell it.

Abandoning and turning back and pushing forward, as if there were no bodies but theirs, dangling from the thundering of what is left of the soul, like two barely visible catastrophes in the wind, touching each other, but not for long; two misfortunes separated since primal times only with the purpose of coming together in brevity; day and night, second and minute, wave and shore. Above this, above this image, above this thought, like a picture hanging above the bed in the sickroom, the undying glory of memory. Memory as it comes to hold the world together. Memory as essentiality. Memory as the clandestineness of life.

When she sleeps, the color of her eyes escapes his mind. And if it were not for the all-too-familiar sounds of the sea, sounds from years ago, sounds from travels not yet planned, sounds from when she is alone in the room and hums the melody of waves to herself; if it were not for the sea, for the black sea, he would perhaps not remember anything at all about this color, this shade, missing from those of his childhood; nothing at all about this whirlwind in the gaze, that nevertheless he would spend hours and hours painting; as light, as flame, as exterior turbulence and remote point in thought.

The walls are closing in, the windows are barring all access, and the wind outside draws his attention to the emptiness of the city streets, to the distant train station and to the many footsteps lost in search of it. A landscape not his own. Something from a book, perhaps; something like an ocean, but not an ocean, a river, crossing in the background, flowing there, right next to the sea, right next to the arteries of the city—magnificent attraction and shelter for the roving eye; it must be a book she loved; something he now paints upon the hour of this swaying, this back-and-forth of the mind as a kind of pleading with the flesh; upon the loneliness of the narrow room, overwhelmed by a remembrance of anything but, by the haze of not knowing whether her eyes are there; whether they themselves are there, or inside an authorial past.

At four in the morning, death comes to mind. Whether this mind belongs to him or to a projection of him, to how she wrote him, how she wrote of him, whether real or reborn, no matter the mind, no matter the body, no matter the materials of the world that they both inhabit, death comes to mind. Death that sends shivers up and down the spine. Ridiculous, inescapable death.

He wishes he could see; he wishes he could know. He wishes he could see her dreams with his eyes, feel them with his body; that he could feel them on his skin, the motion and struggle of these dreams, these explosions of black and white, for that is how she once told him she dreams; sound and image and sometimes stasis; in absence of color, black and white, though he does not remember this either, he does not remember whether it is something she has told him or something he was given as memory. So crucial is this act, this longing, this desire of his to remember, to see beyond the eyelid, to see beyond the sleeping mind, to preempt, to grasp beyond the still-framed soul. It might have been something she said not as a true thing, but as to depict time, to provide an image for a single stretch of time; no colors, for there is no time for time itself to do anything but send her images and dreams and positions like premonitions on the skin; in black and white, when she dreamed, when she woke up; small dismissals of color all over the body. Every way in which she could dream, every way in which she could forget, and remember, and forget again—inscribed, visible, and eventually, erased.

He does not know what she dreams of, yet nonetheless wishes to fall prey to its signification, and so he stays in the room, imagining her at the edge of the sea. Any sea. The black sea. Imagining there the color of her eyes, and in that very moment, this montage of the eternal present.

Twirling around him, the words she has written, these words that have no other place to go, for how could words know when to go—how would they know, when they are made and released into the room, a gushing of ink that does not know where to settle itself—these words that have no mouth to capture, no page to behold; these words that appear as if they themselves were writing, sketching something, shadow puppets, perhaps, shadow puppets on the sheets and on the walls of their narrow room. Textuality at its most intimate.

Abandoned on the shore of his imagination, close to the sinking of the story, close to an end that might have already happened, an end which he is not able to hold into thought for long enough as to become part of this image, for long enough to replace the end she is dreaming, the end she is recreating while she rests. Abandoned there, all matters of the day-to-day. Actions and events and objects that could have been given names, that could have been written and read, that could have been inserted into the story, that could have been brought upon the stage as more than reference of suffocation; these objects, glasses, teapots, shirts and dresses and dissections of a moment, much too reliable to become themselves characters. Abandoned there—everything that she did not write and the whole of what he does not remember, piled up as if to become the flames and ashes of a sacrificial fire.

He tries, and hours pass. He tries, and no color comes

to him. He tries; he thinks of her eyes and of all the times he must have, surely, he must have painted them on the canvas or with letters of black ink; of all the times he must have painted them into the murals of his childhood, like images of the unconscious, from where such a color was absent, the only absent color, the only color the canvas longed for. He tries, he thinks of when she was a stranger, another child in the world. He tries, but death comes to mind again, and he must make time. He must make time and space in the mind for the ending that he is yet unable to grasp as ending.

How to recapture this color? How to create it from nothing when it is absent? How to make of this color an eye, and to this eye to offer another, a companion, so that he himself would then be permitted to have her gaze? How to invent and be part of this process without pulling her from her dreams? How to keep in memory that which is already by his side? How to unobscure the mind?

Having witnessed the creation of other colors, having seen and remembered other eyes, having kept in his memory other gazes, he feels now that this is perhaps a sort of punishment, if not even a betrayal; this, not to remember the color of her eyes, the one sleeping next to him, the one who wanted to be everything at once with him, the one who, in her confrontations with the abject nature of the world, saved him night after night, and will save him again, though salvation is not what he will call it.

Having forgotten this color, the color of her eyes, he thinks to himself that perhaps no other color will ever come, and that no other color is even worth remembering, even though deciding whether to erase their place from his memory, vacant or not, is something he can only do as nothing but writing on the floor, as mere wish, and, if he is to wish for something, he might just wish to remember, rather than to forget. But that is how he embraced life, that is how life came and how he let it wash over him, that is how he made sense of the senseless, and that is where he rooted all his beliefs. To forget is better than to remember.

It came easier to believe in a forgetting, easier to hold on to this act of erasure that had already happened than to wish for remembrance; as so, now, when she slept, he wished to be able to forget all colors, to forget all eyes. He wished for a forgetting as old as time, for something already proved, something that has happened to many, and so it can happen to him; something safe, a forgetting like an embrace, a forgetting that knows not of itself— even though, what then would this forgetting be? He makes an effort to remember. Not her eyes, but reading about forgetting. Reading about how it can provide more solace than memory. Abstracts. Theories. Concepts. Spread across an infinite number of books, plucked from infinite minds; this forgetting, a wave, a fall, arms around the body at night.

There is too much of everything to hold in memory, and he wonders, with this thought—he wonders if there is a way, a proper and practical way to determine whether memory is finite? A way to travel its length, perhaps? A way to reach an edge, and say: This is where memory ends. To look back, and say: This is all that memory can hold. Forgetting has no such borders. There is no limit to how much one can forget. To forget all eyes.

Why this parenthesis? And how might one trust the voice that no longer lives inside a body?

It could be that a future passage of time might provide an answer, perhaps an involuntary depiction of such a voice might come, now, in the narrow room, across nights and seas and in spite of this blindness of the mind that keeps him occupied only so that she could write, and draw, and plan inside her dreams; now, when he gazes at her, sleeping, and finds himself plagued by the impression of forgetfulness, in this series of parallels to another story, to another time, to another life, perhaps, the same, perhaps another interruption of this life, of this story, now, when he looks around the room and rests his head next to her shadow.

He rests his head next to her shadow while thoughts of empty theaters and decaying opera houses take over the body in such a manner that he feels as if flesh is nothing but a manifestation of memory; he feels himself being born, being created, he feels his arms growing and his torso widening, and with each thought he harbors, he feels this even deeper, as if someone were filling his brain with ink and from this ink, he might be able to become again. Himself. As if from this ink comes all forgetting; and from this ink comes also this arm, which he could stretch, this arm with which he could reach and touch her faintly, as to wake her, as to have her open her eyes before him; and from this ink come these fingers, with which to see, fingers like eyes, fingers like projections on the wall.

Eyes like fingers called upon to compose the skin they touch, fingers like eyes called upon to materialize before him the universe of flesh that sleeps beside him; a mass, a body he nevertheless already sees, even though it feels to him that until he is not complete, there can be no body so close, no silence so intimate, no flesh so warm; there can be no impression, even, of such a body, not even a shadow; but if he were not complete, from where these thoughts, from where this guilt at having forgotten?

And if it is she; if she is the author of this world, then she could give him this, she could let him have this, out of kindness, out of necessity, out of love. She could give him the color of her eyes.

SHE FEEDS HIM WORDS. It is morning and they have yet to know what hunger is, but, having slept, having been inside their minds, for so long and so far away, they are now engulfed by a terrible hunger. Possessed by it. Hunger like primal language. Hunger like the simple matter of surviving. Hunger like raw space. Hunger like pain and knowledge and means of expression. Hunger like continuity. Hunger like relation to the self. Hunger like neutrality. Hunger like a bridge to the oneday. Hunger like the erasure of exclusion. Hunger like the exclusion of erasure. Hunger like the already-marked body. Hunger like eternal wish and seduction. Hunger like the shadow of itself, of themselves; hunger like the shadow of all things. Hunger like the yet-unknown. They are famished, and she feeds him words. When the words are gone, she writes more. She writes: When the cold night came, they said, we were not cold, for the Spirit of Fire is our good friend, and she keeps people from perishing. This, a reproduction, words she has read in a book about nature myths, befitting in the moment; these words that she saved for him, from when there was no him, from when she was not the eternal reader; these words that she no longer remembers whether they were assigned to her or if she came upon them in some library, in some foreign city, at the edge of the sea, in a city where the winter wind strikes the face with no other purpose than to remind it of its transience. These words from a book that makes her eyes shine, a sparkle, and then another, just at the thought of it; these words, the bringers of memories from other lives, rediscoveries, reappearances; similar, oh so similar to what she is drawing and writing anew.

She feeds him words, and more words come to her, for she must keep hunger at bay. More words come. Words like migrations inside the heart. Pentimento. She knows still how to recognize a painting erased, replaced; a landscape, any kind of landscape; a body, any kind of body, hidden behind another by the hand of the artist; he told her, he showed her, many times, in the morning and at night, lingering outside the room where he would paint; on the threshold, as he painted, when she too would ask him questions, not needing an answer, question after question, just to be part of that landscape herself, to become an extension of his brush, a resource; thinking that in creating this interaction, in placing her presence there, the hand might paint something that it would not have otherwise painted, not knowing that all that the hand painted were instances of her presence.

This particular truth is something that she must keep: on the threshold, as he painted.

At the very heart of chaos, at the heart of mornings and nights and all that must come to be in order for her to create a world, there lies a hunger that no words could satisfy. Hers. There lies a wish, in conflict with his, and from this conflict, from this chaos, like lightning bolts in the sky, she gazes at and gathers in her arms the very notions that afford this footing. At the very heart of chaos, there are touches and memories of touches; there is abstraction and exposition and expression; there are glimpses of how she must tell this story, of how she must allow others to tell this story, glimpses that remind her of how the storyteller is also a philosopher and the philosopher is also a storyteller—something that comes not to unify all that resides in this chaos, but rather to provide her with a moment to breathe, unrelated to anything and therefore complete. She does not need to define the storyteller— she is not the storyteller. She is the creator of a world already passed. She is the hand that feeds him words.

Their life together was a conventional life. They met at night, like most people, around the corner from a small theater, like most people; they came to know that they

loved each other a few hours later, when it was morning,
like most people; and, like most people, they moved in
together when the walls of the world became so tightening
that no other space seemed to allow for breathing but the
one occupied by the two of them; both of them, at the
same time, in the same space, at night and in the morning;
a space in which to cram all of their possessions, books and
brushes and very few physical representations of the real
world; she did not like to keep photographs and he had
already donated all of the trinkets and vases and old
paintings he was keeping until the night they met, until
the night he walked out of the theater feeling as if everything he had ever touched had something growing on it,
a kind of tumor, something terminal, with each touch;
and not only that, but it seemed to him that these objects
had come together and made a noose around his neck, no,
numerous nooses, endless loops tightening their grip the
more he thought of them, the more he gazed at them and
the more he touched them. His old notebooks, childhood
outfits, his mother's dried-up flowers neatly tucked inside
dozens of envelops, his father's hats and gloves, the six
bicycle wheels that for some reason he had picked up from
the street, saying perhaps to himself that he will one day
make something of them, that he will paint them and
make them nice and give them a purpose again; bicycle
wheels, rusted, bent, ordinary, though not even proper
ones; they were no longer round, they were not circles,

but squares, and maybe they were not bicycle wheels at all. All of these objects, this mass, this paraphernalia, everything was dangling from his neck the night he exited the theater too absentmindedly to see that his steps were taking him around the corner, toward forgetting, toward rebirth.

They dangled and tightened and made loud noises as they touched each other and he felt, placing one heavy foot in front of the other, he felt as if the world, the whole of the world was hearing this noise, this scream, this echo of being weighed down; as if every single person in the world could see these trinkets dangling from his neck, tugging, pulling his head to the ground. He saw this, on the face of each and every stranger passing by, he saw a kind of pity, some sort of compassion, though he himself no longer knew how to feel nor how to recognize it, but there was something, a way for him to look and see and call it compassion; and seeing it turned his blood into ice, a frozen misery, not one that paralyzes, but one that echoes and says: You are cold, you are growing colder, and the more you carry, the colder you will become; the more bicycle squares around your neck, the more ice will form and crack and travel through your arteries to find its way into the heart.

A terrible image, he thought, ignoring the fact that he himself was the one who had created such an image. A terrible vision, that of ice traveling through the body, not metaphorically, not splinters of ice as figures of literary illustriousness or manners of speaking; this journey, not as an exposé before one's eyes, not as scenery that lives in the mind, and even there not as an epitome of something else. No, real ice traveling through the veins, real ice piercing the heart, real ice growing, the more he gathered, the more he painted, the more he kept, the more he remembered, the more he attempted to be a part of life. Real ice, the more he breathed.

But yes, their life together was a conventional life. They lived, like most people. They breathed, and kissed, and embraced one another, at night, and in the morning, like most people. They boiled water and made coffee or tea or nothing at all, like most people. They read to one another and wrote short messages which they then hid for the other to find. They made a message of their bodies. They baked bread and cut fruit into odd shapes only to abandon them on the counter as they followed this or that craving, like most people. They detested themselves one without the other, like most people. They went out and walked the streets for days; they followed a reverie, an urge, a journey plucked from the depths of a dream they both had as children, like most people. They trembled and echoed and became exacerbation, and moment, and climacteric intercourse, like most people. They watched films and later spoke of these films and from them, they sometimes chose the simplest one, the most banal, and they would watch and watch until they knew this film by heart and then they would forget it and they would watch it again, like most people. They spoke of reality as a means to prevent it from suffocating them; they made from understanding and intimacy a path out of the world, like most people. They fantasized images of ordinary togetherness but also images of death embraced, images of cruelty upon those who they thought were hurting the realm of all things, those making it impossible for them to live in the world by themselves. Like most people.

Sometimes they would not return to the apartment for weeks. Other times, the apartment was a house, and while this made it even more difficult to leave it, for they had there everything two people might need, two people who do not need very much when they are one in the gaze of the other, there were still days, weeks, when they would leave and not return until one of them remembered something abandoned at home: a notebook that needed filling, a sheet that she had left on the bedroom floor that needed folding, a book with its last pages left unread, a corner of a room that had not yet been painted blue.

Sometimes what they would return for was something neither of them gave name to, something that might not even exist as an object or action or event in the world. Other times, they would return for what they already had, for things they could find whenever, wherever; but they needed to return. They needed to hear the sound of the door closing behind them; the door to the apartment, the door to the house, they needed to hear it open and close, like a gesture of rebellion against the whole of the outside, and then and only then could they—could he run his fingers through her hair and put his arms around her and while doing so, gaze up at the ceiling to see there the murals of cathedrals from other times. It was he who needed to return. It was she who gave him the possibility of this return. And to both of them, their room, their home, whatever, wherever; image or drawing or simple line in a poem; home as the streaming of the inside, home as the gushing of all blue.

But since he could not tell her this, since he had decided that he will never speak of this to her, he would make up strange and often silly reasons that she had no choice but to listen to; no choice but to return, sometimes out of sheer curiosity, to see him at home, to see him wrapped in his routine in the morning, for she did not know, but there was something in the way he would ask her, something in the way in which he often pleaded for a return, without ever there being a reason for pleading; something that told her that they must go home, that she must go, and give him this, whatever it was, whatever the reason he would put his arms around her differently when they were there and it was but the two of them. Simply because it was the strongest of attractions, the warmest of loves. Holding oneself and holding the Other. Becoming center and void, presence and absence; and everywhere, at any time, the home of all things, the home of all bodies, the home of two humans, the lonely ones, the ones developed in thought, on canvas, and from letters on the floor.

She feeds these words to him now, these memories, words like the hours of the clock; she offers them to him in the best shape she herself can retrieve them, as best as she can muster, for when these words, when these memories return, even into this body that is but an image of her body, when they invade even this double of what was once her real self, she cannot but feel taken by ice through the veins, his ice; and from this ice comes a trembling no writing hand can survive; and so she does it carefully, she feeds him fragments of their conventional life with enough care as not to bring it all back. And then, returning to an earlier thought, she wonders, Can one do so in writing? The room suddenly empty, in another time, in another year, almost as if the real had returned. Can one replace a landscape, a body, any body, if one were to hide it behind another, same as one would a painting?

But writing is not writing as the real ones knew it; now, for them, writing is throwing oneself thought-first into the waves of the devouring sea, the waves of this memory, something she missed as she was writing, a thought, a revelation, an understanding that she lacked, as she wrote more and more words to stave off hunger.

An exercise. This: to be devoured and survive. An appeal to movement; an emphasis on withdrawal as continuity; words, taken from one mouth to the other, from one hand to the other, from the human to the reinvented, from the one who writes to the one who needs to be rewritten. And it is through this exercise that conflict surfaces. Another kind of conflict, perhaps for the first time. In this sequence, of the one who needed to be rewritten; a sequence, not a body, not a person; it is here that she sees: such knowledge never existed. There never was this image, the full, graspable image of the one she is now writing and feeding and keeping alive through the blue of her heart. There never was something so complete that she could take and create from it a whole person, the same person, with the same face and the same love on the tongue; the same person, with the same organs in the body and the same labyrinth in the mind.

There never was, and so what she is doing, what she is keeping alive is pure thought, the faltering of language, something she told herself she must do from the second absence settled. There is life in death, and after death, there is life if one knows how to breathe it into a new body, any kind of body; a written one, even; a body of paper and memories of conventional life; a body like a message of life; and, why not, a body of autumn rustle and cemeteries and theaters that never stay open until that close to midnight. There is life and there are ways. This, in her eyes: an act of love.

BLUE HAS RETURNED OUTSIDE THEIR WINDOW, and, with his arms around her, their faces now dissolved together, in this, his final year, when they are but a mass of flesh, when they are but this marvel of blue, when, within and without, they are but the separation to come, he thinks of prophets from the past and how they spoke of the spirit in such a way that he almost believed — no, he did believe — in such a way that it made him grow a spirit of his own, a soul, something invisible for the heart to carry and protect, something white, perhaps, or red, or blue; this blue outside, the blue of other years, the bluest of blues; something for the body to carry and the mind to use as companion. The weight-bearing spirit unto all paths. An invention, nonetheless, but an invention vital to the body, an invention cherished by the eye, an invention like an urge of the senses. From this point on, the spirit, the soul, that which resided inside the heart, entirely primitive, primal, feral, worn-out by the ways of the world, exhausted by the whole that knew not of its fragments; the spirit, the soul, a memory, a trace, a rigor, a blanket upon the bones, a leaning against the wall. The spirit, a requirement of experience, of life, of the many displays of life; a concept unto itself, a concept that nevertheless grew flesh and limbs and learned to walk and search and find all things; things it would gather and hide inside the heart. For him, this spirit, which he would search for not within himself but inside of books and the thoughts of those on whom he leaned for comfort, this spirit brought him the simplest of joys. That of existence that did not need to be demonstrated. The joy of being without visibility, the joy of existing without needing to. The joy of something that lives inside the body as the body itself. Something that invited thoughts of all kinds. Cannibalism. Tenderness. Punishment. Caregiving. Acceptance. Suffocation. Reflection. Attraction. Loathing. Something there, for him to have as double, before knowing that there are ways, that there are other ways to become two, other ways to remain in the world, other ways to be loved, and present, and eternally tied to the glorification of presence. This spirit, this soul — she would rather catch glimpses of it in art than in books. As art. She felt something akin to discomfort when reading about it, when hearing from words and phrases how there is something; something to be loved, something to be carried; how there is a soul, a spirit, something at the heart of all things carnal, at the root of all corporeality; how there is something, and this something, was never the same in all words, and so she felt discomfort when reading about it.

She preferred art. Though not the whole of art. Not art as concept, not art as universality, not art as balm. She preferred individual works of art. To gaze upon them and find in them traces of what the eye would never be able to otherwise see, unless through metaphor and struggle and invention. Individual works of art. Less studied, less known, those works of art on the verge of erasure, as they themselves are, as they find themselves now, their faces dissolved together; this mass of blue on the verge of existence. Perhaps, yes, in a painting of a woman scratching her arm; perhaps there, and perhaps this: the chiaroscuro of disruption; same as she found in his first paintings; even when there is nothing to disrupt, even when nothing is visible; more so when nothing is visible. If she wanted to grasp the spirit, the soul, she would go and encounter these works of art, these executions, these massacres on canvas. For her, this meeting, this search, took on the role of a substitution—it became the eye itself. It became the mind. It became the writing hand. In truth, the way in which she encountered these slivers of all that is invisible inside the body was nothing more than a turning against herself, for she could have very well closed her eyes and imagined. She could have closed her eyes and imagined what lay inside her, what it was that rested at the core of her existence, but no, she preferred to catch glimpses of it in art.

In art, in the painting of a woman. A glimpse, a turn of

the head, and the arm is revealed. Another, and cascading blonde hair fills the narrow room. At last, this final frame, enchanted and ethereal: the white gown, flowing to the floor in waves and pleats. And it comes to her now, disrupting the very thought of disruption, interrupting this descent of the spirit unto canvas, she remembers a clothesline of white dresses, nothing but white dresses, so many that the clothesline becomes a river and flows into a sea of white. With each glimpse, with each memory of these fabrics, of their shapes and fastenings and their tiny buttons, with each memory, the image gains new powers of alienation, utterly catastrophic in their eloquence. Something of excessive presence, for other years and other shadows. Something wounding, for her, in other times.

His great concern, not during the course of his illness, but in the years before, having just met, having just found this manner of living, the lateness of it, his great concern was then the gap between things. Almost as something manifesting before him. Sometimes, when walking, he would recalibrate his steps to avoid this gap, as if he were marking a dark zone, visible to him alone, tracing it with the light of his eyes, illuminating it so he could see, precisely, what was hiding inside of it, if anything. Why the gap between things? Why this confluence of mind and gap? Why this interest? And what exactly was it that qualified as such? What were these things that separated themselves one from the other, that made space for a gap to form? It wasn't that such a separation rattled him. Nor was he interested in it as a kind of study. Maybe that would have made it simpler. More formalized. It would have made it easier for the heart to know and the intellect to understand. More so, if he too could have gazed at art and find in it depictions, representations and interpretations of this schism—he, the painter, after all—if he could have found there the gap between things, the breaking down of boundaries, if he could have been given this opportunity, to see, to compare, to know, he would have been able to make of this thought a full one. A circle. But his sources were literal. Philosophical. The written word, in all forms. Poetry. Exegesis. It was in the word and through the word that he managed to capture this separation, its colors and its light, the dark that stood at its edges. In the word and through the word that he found ways to paint, ways to let the hand do as it pleased, ways to think of the body and of nature, ways to depict them on canvas, ways to rebel against the gap between things. In the words she read to him and through the words she fed him, he found movement, and context, and color; he found the gleaming of flesh and the blue of the outside world. Being at home under the blue of the sky. And no matter what he painted, it came from words, and it came from her presence. No matter what kind of growing apart, he would make sense of it through phrases and chapters and sentences she would sometimes leave for him around the room, chapters and phrases and sentences for him to examine, to break down and draw from them the very nature of the unconscious, to pull from them the inner compulsion of the gap that forms itself between all that there is.

One might think that there was an impossibility to this correspondence. To the manner in which they completed each other, but in an odd fashion, that there is nothing conventional in their conventional living, that he paints what cannot be painted and she writes what cannot be written, and together, they might make of this impossibility a living, a way of life; that they are deliberately cultivating this lack, and breaking the world into small pieces just so there is more for them to devour. One might say that to want and to become is a kind of experiment that they had failed at, or simply that their strange representation of things is nothing to concern oneself with, that there are lives and means to live them that should not be manifested unto the eternal. That the death of something senseless is a death one should accept. And maybe if the story had space for other elements, if the stage itself were not so cluttered, if the night were not brimming, then a senseless something might become the sense of something. Between this thought and any other, between the attempt at understanding why them and why like this, and the desire to get swept away by the flow of their life together, therein lies precisely the gap he so adamantly wanted to make sense of. A marvelous action, to fall, to collapse atop what one contests. To become prey and to do so with infinite pleasure. To discover, and through this discovery to find that no act is more sublime than the one born from the unknown, from the conventional that verges on maddening the very world that deemed it as such. No act more sublime than to free oneself and free the Other. As for the viewer, for the stage, for the possibility of creating, for the mural and the blue, for departing from the senses and the connotations of a brushstroke, no attempts at visualization and understanding should be made from the whole without the fragment, without all of its fragments. One can go further and speak of the eternal, and how it would then be impossible to grasp all the fragments of a whole, when there is eternity, when there is repetition, when nonlinearity is absent and all that one is given is everything, but as chaos, as rupture and rapture; chaos as the medium itself.

He thinks, We are dying. An echo of her words from earlier in the day, as she uttered them to herself when circling similar obstacles as the ones before him now, truths that might have once been essential to her very existence, truths that became particles of ink, nothing but particles of ink on the page. Earlier in the day, earlier in the year, earlier. We are dying.

The exacting ways in which they interacted with each other and with the objects around them, the ways in which they became conscious of this interaction, of the fact that even in absence, even in silence, there remained a touch; there remained the manner in which they touched, the manner in which they held one another and everything around them—these ways often returned to him as shadows of intentionality, as linguistic acts and presences of a past he no longer knew nor wanted to hold in grasp. He thought then about continuity. Continuity in how he saw the world. Continuity in seeing the world. Continuity in this guilt, this remorse, this regret at feeling the past slip from his hands precisely because of intentionality. He thought, and wondered, how it was that it came to be, this unreal landscape of abandonment, how it came to be that he wished to look around and see nonbeing, how it came to be that he wished for shadows, and darkness, and the coldness of nontouch. He still carries the miniscule projector in his pocket, day after day, night after night. He carries it and asks her, sometimes only through gestures, through cranings of the neck as if to point toward the place where he might project it, what is it that she wishes to see next, though they never use it, though they never see any films, not anymore; yet through this lack of image, they gain somehow a vision of eternal skin, glowing, languishing in the aftermath of an oneiric touch, a vision like the chronogram of the fall of angels.

Sometimes he leaves notes for her in which he writes of his dreams. Notes like living arrangements. Notes like portraits. Notes like autumnal testimonies. Other times, they are letters; long, beautiful, detailed letters, even when she might be standing beside him as he writes them, even when she might be gazing over his shoulder and see then the movement of his hands and recognize in them a message to her: *Yours.* When he knows that she will not interrupt him, when he keeps on writing, these letters, these notes, these small confessions—these ways of the flesh, one after the other.

Letters in which he speaks of his dreams, of what he sees in them, what he makes of them; of running along the only way possible; of how he hurts, of how he hurts her. Everything. He begins a sentence and writes it all, knowing, fearing—knowing that the time he has left, the time to dream and the time to write of dream is not limited, but already passed. Knowing that this time belongs to another, something that he himself cannot erase, and yet also something that cannot remove him from life; something like a knowledge of life, that life never felt more like life; proper life, this life, with all that there is, with the meager and the bountiful, with nothing now to hang around his neck, now that this very truth, told in reverse, that this time is not his own time, and that the life he had barely learned how to live was fading with each new dream, with each new letter, with each new morning when the sun would come and tell him, when the sun would come and teach him another way of counting the hours, a way of having two instead of one, a way of turning the two into four. Knowing all this, he begins a new letter.

No matter the hours, no matter how many, no matter how time passes, no matter conflicting forces, no matter sensations, of any kind; no matter life and no matter the blue outside their window, what is meant to pass has passed, and in its passing, she has found the means to make it eternal. Through expression, through imagery, through writing and drawing and circling nature and paradises; from twisting the arms of time, from everything and anything. A path, a possibility, a manner of living, an abuse of dying. Then and only then will she close her eyes and see, and find there, behind the dark of her eyelids—then and only then will she see there, playing on a loop, in the five days that will pass from the first snow of the year, from the last breath, she will find there another possibility; the possibility of creating something, a raft, something to keep her floating happily on the surface of the sea; something, someone, to come and be him; someone living, but altogether him.

In this final year, when the time spent together multiplied, for him, while becoming scarcer and scarcer for her, they forgot, both of them, little by little or all at once, they forgot how to leave the apartment, the house, the massacre, how to spend days and weeks chasing something; a rush, a craving, a path, a film on the walls of the city. They forgot. The longest film was yet to come.

The longest film was yet to be projected, by hands and snowfall and eternity as it comes and falls like a veil over one's eyes; over her eyes; the eternity it took for the hand to be covered by the white of snow, for the hand and the scar and the memory of touch to be buried with the body. The longest film she ever saw, something that felt, then, in the graveyard, like a creation of the mind, a hallucination, something created and projected at the same time, that delay of snow, that blanket of white that unfolded and unfolded, that grew larger and larger, wider and wider, always missing those few inches of skin, the skin of his left hand, as if there was enough warmth there to melt all the snow in the world—there, in the scarring of tissue, there, where no amount of snow would ever be able to fall and cover it. It felt like that, in those eternal seconds. An illusion, of course, for enough snow did fall, and the body was buried, and the hand along with it.

December, when snow falls and travels to the very chambers of the heart, when it travels and settles itself there, making it cold enough for her to harvest it as ink, cold enough for that to offer her the blue, all the blue, enough blue as to create the whole of time, not as return, but as eternity; there, inside a narrow room, on the floor and on the walls of this narrow room. Cold enough and blue enough for them to live a conventional eternity. A vast, pulsating eternity. To touch, briefly and forever, to touch voices and skin and objects around the neck without having these voices, this skin, these objects, without having them be anything other than extended pleasures of the mind and of the body. Cold enough for the hand to be recreated, repositioned, to be given a place of repose, a proper place, somewhere to settle, and rest, and warm itself; on the throat, on the thigh, along the curves of the body; anywhere on the body, now eternal—the body, now able to sustain the very erasure of death. Cold enough for the narrow room to become a natural extension of the world, frozen in time and in space, frozen inside of the bluest of hearts, not like a disease that needs to be cured, but like the second heart one grows when one is granted the means to grow it.

Cold enough for the collapse to be a coming together. Cold enough for passion. Cold enough for apocalypse and chaos to take on the unfolding of characters in a novel; actors on the stage; roles one can write and direct and form to one's liking. Cold enough for twisted perspectives to become realities and invented bodies to become real bodies and bodies of work. Cold enough.

THERE WERE TIMES when he would make her speak incessantly. Anything, he would say. Tell me about birds. Tell me about the pain of killing a bird. Tell me about drawings and imposed pleasures. Tell me about the cinema, and the image, and a day filled with impossibilities. Tell me if you were ever a child. Yes, if she was ever a child, like he once was, if she ever gazed so high up that the neck felt as if it would break and make the head roll off the body. If she was ever a child, like he was, and, in cathedrals, if she ever looked up at the artificial, the painted sky, for hours and hours, so many hours that the real sky became the artificial one, so many hours that the eyes became the carrier of clouds. So many hours that no real stars could match the beauty of these paintings seen there, in cathedrals and museums and opera houses, places that no child wished to visit, places that for him were the whole of the universe crammed inside a single gaze. If death ever came and wrapped her arms around you. This, a premature question, as it would have been for any living being, to be asked — to be asked and to have to answer. Tell me if there was ever another *you*.

Her fascination with these moments when no echo was too loud and no denial too significant grew deeper with each new question. If only she could have him speak like that every month, every day; if she could have him there, and here, and anywhere, in every minute of their conventional life together, asking her questions about birds, she might find in that a thread to spin herself anew into the ways of the world, and through this spinning, she might perhaps recapture the strength to keep only what needs to remain. Without this strength, there was nothing but to reinvent the whole of the world. Nothing but to let the new world unfold as it may.

His question, no matter where they would find them-selves, whenever it would come, remained a metaphysical given. There was the question, and nothing more. Every-thing else needed to be created time and time again, needed to be earned. The question, occurring in a kind of natural state, as if part of nature itself. His question, supplementing all insufficiencies, asserting all manners of living, directing toward all paths at once. His question. Tell me about the death of birds.

The sequence of lives as if seen on film clouds her mind forcing circles to be drawn by invisible hands at unhuman speed, forcing ruptures and departures from the once-lived, and so nothing that she can think of saying will ever please the memory of those moments. She feels this, and for this, she is silent. These are lives that she does not know, after all, she has never seen these birds, she has never traveled these paths. It all takes place in the mind, and it does so with the swiftness of a history being written on the body in decay, when they touch, when it is night, and he pushes her away, but the room is too narrow and the walls return her into his embrace. When there is power between them, but they both delegate it to the void. They don't want the other to feel impelled in any way. Living as they live, in this codependence, they are both aware that if one were to be more than the other, everything would fall apart. And so they dissipate power, they dissipate any feeling that is more potent than another, into the abyss, into the gaps that form themselves between things in the room. There are many, and they are filled with endless torments.

For her, it becomes a matter of writing. She questions how it would be to write of it. If one were to put this trans-formation into words, this practice, this language; to write of it and write with it; this spectacle of life that she sees unraveling chaotically before and around her, like the pages of a book without a spine, a book that is no longer a book but a masterpiece of corporeality, a body that has not yet learned how to be *body*; if one were to write of these unknown lives—unlived, even, for she does not know if these are birds or dreams, if these are bodies falling to the ground or little renunciations of the mind, denials and rejections and refusals of the real; she does not know if what comes now, when he asks her another one of his questions, if what flows between them as if from a consciouness outside of themselves, from something that harbors the thoughts and desires of anyone who has ever lived, and returns them to those

    with grief, she does not know if all this is what she herself sees and feels, or if it is her mind telling her it wishes to lose itself into the web of a world that once was— if one were to write of these lives, it would have to be on the very passage of time.

Metempsychosis, she answers, without remembering the question. The death of birds.

It must be one of his memories, it comes to her, when the question returns, and just as the words roll off the tongue, she remembers also that through this and through this alone she can keep him like he always was, through answering his eternal questions, his morning and his midnight questions, can they themselves become eternal. She must have answers. She must herself become the answer.

In the meantime, she must write. When placed alongside his memories, that which he has shared with her, when brought together with fragments from his real life, this writing takes on the shape of an endlessness not even she is familiar with. A borne desire. It is in moments like these that she understands him better, though not enough as to cave in to the same belief, when she understands why he struggled, why he longed to end endlessness, why so many of their conversations centered around this one thought: that no matter the promise, no matter the potentiality, there is nothing there for him to hold on to, there is nothing in the vision of a life eternal that he would want, and he knew, as soon as he would utter it, that it hurt her terribly to contemplate it, though at the root of things, and before, before him, before his illness, before the first snow of the year, when she was indeed someone else, then, there was no aspiration toward the eternal in her mind either, and when she would think of this, she would only do so as abstract thought.

Now, in the rocking chair, in her black dress, folding and unfolding a piece of paper, one of their notes, perhaps, all she could think about was how to create and preserve and thrive in the eternal. How to be herself the question and the answer and the very breath between them.

From other years, as if sent to salvage the mind from the cruelty of the thoughts it had begun to harbor, comes his voice, the echo of words forgotten yet so familiar.

And now? Forgive me if I do not say enough. Have you forgiven me?

He pauses. The story remains unperverted.

There is, high above, on the ceiling of the room, something like a faded painting, the relic of what he once painted there, when the uttered these words, words she no longer recalled until they returned as if by miracle, though even now, she is unable to make sense of them enough as to remember what he was referring to. More so now, in the narrow room, when living inside an invention, when mirrored, when doubled, when recreated, when there are no memories let alone memories of disagreements or disputes, memories of what might demand forgiveness. Every desire must be uttered. Every desire, an exaltation. There, on the ceiling of the room, something from which to recreate the world, a blue into which to dip one's fingers and make with it mouths and lips and voices that speak and say that the question carries within its own answer, that the answer is not substance, not individuality, but beginning and end and the whole of the in-between. There, high above, in ruin, half-erased, the way through which to unveil the whole of everything, to unveil it for enough time as to make from this sight, from this seeing, to make from it a character in the story, an actor

on the stage, a role on the page, to make from it a manifestation of love, and from this love, to birth the eternal.
The meaning of life aligned with that of death. Two
humans, from the ruins of a mural on the ceiling, the
lonely ones, the only ones.

She cannot breathe. Suddenly, she cannot breathe.
She writes, still, she writes and writes, but she can no
longer breathe. Without any idea whatsoever as to why,
without nothing to claim significance, without any
impulse but to destroy, to break away from the invisible
hands that have reached from somewhere and are now
tightening their grip around her throat, she tries to pause,
to retreat into a different corner of the room, to find there
something neutral, something soothing, something illuminating; to shed light and find what it is that birthed this
insufficiency of breath. To go where there is air. But her
hands do not listen, and language itself becomes hostile;
her hands do not stop writing, they do not listen to the
body; her left hand does not touch the forehead, as it
usually does, it does not touch the forehead nor does it
descend to trace the line of her face, down to the neck that
throbs and spasms as it does when she is unwell and in
search of ways of soothing the mind for however long the
body needs to recover. Language itself becomes something
that suffocates, and there is more and more of it, there are
more words and more images of these words, there are

reasonings yet never one she could use to free herself, and the hand does not stop writing and there are more and more words, more hostilities and more visions. There is less and less breath.

No, her left hand remains there, writing, creating, piecing together limbs and torso, thought and mind, touch and response; it stays there drawing the arteries of the world that cannot live without this gesture, and so all other gestures have been erased not just from her mind but also from the memory of her fingers; her fingers that used to travel as if to take her pulse, though she never counted, in fact, never paid much attention to what the hand was doing, for there was barely any breath and nothing helped but this, to allow herself this falling into a haze, to allow herself to be engulfed by a kind of fog that veiled the eyes and the reasoning of all thought, a dizziness that nonetheless provided the body with a measure of comfort, with the coming of a presence, with enough comfort for the breath to slowly return back to normal, for the redness to leave her cheeks. She was not pale, she would not become pale when she would get like this, when she could not breathe; no, she would turn red, vermillion, and warm, and it was always as if one could see the tiny veins carrying blood through the caverns of her head, almost as if one could see them begging to break open the skin, needing to escape, these tiny specks of vermillion red, once blue; these veins so narrow and so small, always invisible in other times.

The infinity of these colors, through the skin, through the mind, coursing through the narrow room and filling it with a reality not given, but recreated.

She keeps on writing and more questions come. Questions she does not know how to answer but questions she answers nonetheless, for she knows there must always be an answer. She must. She herself is the answer. She keeps on writing. The corpus remains constant.

Outside, by means of anamnesis, the feverish pursuit for the last day goes on undisturbed. It will come and it will bring with it the first snow of the year.

She must repeat this to herself, for the timeline is not linear, it is out-of-focus and obscure and at times buried in snow, it is expression and gesture, always veiled by something else, and even if it were, even if there were no blurriness, the mind would not be able to hold in grasp the whole of everything. The mind needs repetition, and reawakening; the mind needs to have answers and words and lines and circles; and ink, yes, sufficient ink with which to create and forgive and always remember. Enough ink to consider all aspects, enough ink to draw all contours, enough ink to give life to each and every second of their time together. Enough ink to afford more time, an infinity of new seconds, though this, she has not yet mastered, how to create newness, something that does not gush forth from what was, something that comes and rises on its own, though in thinking it, she forgets that in the narrow room, the lonely ones, the only ones, she forgets that they have found new ways, that they see each other with other eyes, and love each other with other resonances. She forgets that the hands that touch are not the hands covered by snow, that that which she calls senses, the senses she has called into rebecoming, she forgets that they are senses made anew, that they are senses without knowledge, without retention, senses without the memory of a past touch.

As a remedy, as a manner of breathing, she takes this: repetition does not compromise the work, repetition does not come as malformation of the body. And yet, repetition is not newness, and the *body of work* cannot provide its own interpretation unless there is a presence to grasp it. As remedy, she gives herself more, something intensely intimate, something healing: there are ways. There are ways, and *the word* is still theirs. The landscape is alive, it breathes and reaches and wishes to touch; the room is narrow enough as to hold everything together. The words are many, and brimful. They birth other words. There are ways. Ways unto themselves, ways like rights and laws of living, ways like connections, ways from mouth to ear, ways from voice to heart, ways yielding the invention of invention itself. There are ways, and she has gathered them all.

THROUGH THE APPEARANCE OF A NEW WORLD, it comes into being, this dialogue, in the pattering rain, considerations upon the pavement, rain unusual for this time of year, which she takes as proof that earthly life remains unfettered, that human reality exists anywhere and everywhere, that nothing disintegrates as tradition would have it; this dialogue now in a low register voice, almost as if both of them would rather be silent, this dialogue comes like a paradoxical scream into her confused hearing. A scream that plunges her into the depths of the darkest of nights, a scream that pierces and hurts and angers all the more because it is not rightly remembered, because it comes as argument yet again, as shattering of the windows of the room; and she says to herself that she maybe has mistakenly brought together the words of this conversation from so many versions of the past that what she has now created is a terrible disagreement, yet one they never had, an argument the two invented humans are having, without knowing what it is that they are saying to each other, without knowing what it is that they are writing, on the floor and on the walls, an argument that saddens them, without knowing how to be sad. It comforts her. The thought that this scream comes from nowhere. That is all she can say.

If eternity were to all of a sudden become not real, but widely accepted, if the world were to embrace the existence of something beyond, not as afterworld, not as stillness, but as continuity, as life as one knows it, as consciousness, and motion, and realization of the real within the eternal, if all of this were to be confronted and embraced, one morning, as if it had always been part of the realm of all things—she thought for a second how easy it would become, a much-too-brief second in which she allowed the perception of this thought: that leaning on universality, on the help of others, on voluntary gusts of wind and sympathetic waves of the sea, would make it possible for her to create without exhaustion, possible to rest; yet as swiftly as it came, the thought is lost to her own reality, lost to slivers from their life together, lost to a cord of the senses that passes through both of them, through the room, through the whole of time; lost to brushstrokes and lines and phrases excluding, separating themselves from a reality that would make them identical parts of the world. The disappearance of this thought passed through her and left a terrible cold within.

Colder than anything, colder than time not allowing rebecoming, colder than infinite distance, colder than everything that might drive one to walk the streets at night in search of negations and manners of being. Colder than death. She felt ashamed at thinking this thought. Ashamed at inviting this possibility, and the more she felt it, the less it appeared to her that such a reality would be anything but injurious. By one and the same stroke, she had lost everything she had ever gained, and gained everything she had ever lost.

    With her fingers and her arms and the whole of her body covered in ink stains and in the wounds of writing, for too long and in too-tight a space, she pauses and thinks of signs outside of bodies. She thinks of signs and in this thinking lies a desire to return to a previous state of existence. She thinks of how there have been days, months, years, perhaps, time in which she has not gathered signs as she once did; she wonders what might have happened with these signs, in her absence, when she was not there to greet them, she wonders whether these signs might have still found their way to her; whether they might be in the words she has written, whether they are the very particles of ink she used to write them; whether she even needs these signs, now, when the whole of existence is in her control, now, when all that there is is the word, and in it lie all connections past and connections to come. Too many associations for her to grasp, too many for her to gather and then set free on the floor of the narrow room and call them literature; the literature of a life together. Now, when ink has marked her as much as she has marked everything with ink, she no longer needs signs.

She herself has become the sign and symbol of a promise. She herself has become what makes the sign a sign, what is attributed to hidden meaning and furtive gazes at that which resides beneath the surface of things. These signs, real or imagined, she has become them, they are all over the skin, they are resting amidst her organs, they are the thoughts in her head, they are this play at literature and the reinvention of real life that is to exhaust her for years to come. She knows this, and she positions herself just so that she takes on the shape of—by virtue of light and reflection—the shape of the ruin of these signs, the shape of the ruin of these signs.

Would it not be wonderful? To disintegrate and become absence. To become the omnipotence of love. She falls asleep like this, thinking of such a love, albeit in contradiction with the rest of her world; a pleasing contradiction that will remain in the background of her ways for as long as there are ways. Something without figure, without a proper shape that she might later draw or write about on the floor and in notes to leave around the room. A contradiction that often takes on the role of the narrative voice. A contradiction that questions the very need for the eternal. Simple, gracious, inviting, a contradiction that comes and goes, that empties and fills; a contradiction like an intrusion of the senses, like that which conceals transgression. A contradiction like a torment of language, like a contortion of the body, like the ruin of all memory.

From the first pages of her work, her *body of work,* her work as actual body, what stands out, to herself and to anyone who might consult them, is the nature of the coldness from which she pulls the properties of space and time. There, in her first pages, one can find a detailed account of how she will manage this, albeit hidden, unwritten, left to the imagination, but nonetheless present: an account of how to mimic the laws of space and time, not laws as one knows it, but as new decrees; preceding and succeeding any others; as chaos and rearrangement of all that is natural, and human, and aberrant; a physical rearrangement, concealed in ink, one that will permit her to create, to re-create the whole of a world.

The laws of space and time, of sex and death, of absence and presence, of self and the Other, of blue and horizons; the very laws of love and how this love lingers upon the skin; of consciousness and finitude and wonder and eroticism; of desire in concealment and desire as revelation.

To this end, to the making of this world, as she once knew it, as she now needs it, she has reconsidered everything else. To keep present, and unchanged, and eternal what she needs in order to survive, she had to reconsider and restage and misshape the whole of everything. Plunging her hands into the space where everything overlapses, she creates there, she pulls from there new manners of being. She pulls from there the *beyond*, the *something else*, the *evermore*. The grasp and the subjugation, the silk and the rope, the crucified and the resurrected.

With her hands deep in this space, she learns, she re-learns how to make of the *I* a pure philosophical idea, and from this idea she extracts a new being, a double of herself, someone to live and breathe in the narrow room, someone to write and feed him, someone to write of life and destruction, someone to live without the existence and question of a god, and yet to pray; to pray each day, to pray at night, to pray not as one prays, but with the body, with the mouth, to pray with fingers on ribs beneath the skin. A paradise in which two humans live; two new beings, a place of emission, of release, a place where two humans live, oblivious to any perspective other than that of life inside the narrow room. To assume that death made all of it possible: what inconceivable pleasure.

Every December, he asks her another question. A question that does not lead anywhere but to the understanding of this month. The last month of the year. A question that serves to further life. The drive toward a repetition that denies its definition. A distinctive question, never the same, a question different from the questions of other months; a question that sometimes even alters the premise of all those other questions; one that is formulated just so she knows that it is December, formulated so she can tell there is something denoting about this question, even though the words themselves, even though the question itself is rarely anything significant, even though it almost never stays with her after she has answered it; but somehow, in his voice, in everything that surrounds him, that surrounds them, she can hear that it is December, the month itself meaningless to both of them. Within this question, the whole of their existence, the tendency toward the Other, toward being in the Other, in this question, everything that pertains to love and everything that abides by no rules, not even those made by themselves, for themselves and for the world.

On his deathbed, just as he planned it, it will be December, and he will ask her a final question. One last question for her to answer, something like a touch, a question whose memory she will not hold, something like a ravishment, of the mind and of the body. She does not remember how she answered this question, she does not know what it was that she said, nor the relation between *question* and *answer*; she does not remember whether her answer pleased him, whether his question saddened her. It remains an act of speech that has escaped from memory. And with this forgetting come the ghosts of other forgettings, of each and every forgetting she had to allow for her act of life to be what she needed it to be, the ghosts of everything she brushed away to make room for all this newness. This newness as orgasmic union. This newness as openness, as tree and flower, as otherness, as existence. This newness, as adoration. As the knowledge of movement. This newness that came with such effort. This newness, as a detour to death.

She does not remember the final question, nor the answer, nor the adoration that rose between them in that moment, and in its place; she writes of previous Decembers, she writes of the questions and answers of other years, of how they would linger outside in the freezing air, when she would see something in the street, something not meant to be alive in winter, and remain there, in its presence, until they were both terribly cold. She writes of these questions and answers, and also, she writes of all other questions, of different understandings and memories and self-interruptions that lived before their very existence; she writes as if to create now, on a single page, on the infiniteness of this one page, a glossary of everything he had ever asked her and everything she had offered in return, and from it, to create a new language, a language that can be held by the tongues of the dead. A language that sustains itself through death, and life, and the desire to be born anew.

Anything, everything, just to preserve the illusion of continuance, for there cannot be new life, and there cannot be a new body, without the existence of these questions, before death reenters the world, and so she writes, now and every day, in every hour, she writes more and more questions for herself; some retrieved from memory, others pulled from the vastness of what she wishes he had asked her, or from the emptiness of what she suspects he had planned on asking her, later, if the years would have been many, and the questions would have needed to multiply themselves accordingly. She writes, and the text itself becomes a pleasure of the body, of the mind; it becomes breath and respite and the virtue of all that is sacred.

She writes and she is in awe of the immortality of these shared moments, of the infiniteness of question and answer, lack and knowledge, self and the Other. She is in awe and she wonders whether what she is inscribing, whether these questions would come to him in the moment he would ask them or if they were there from before, brewing; a theory of recollection; whether he had been formulating them inside the mind, for days, months in advance, or whether there had been something about her, something in her gestures, something only attained when there is a gesture and a body to carry it; something in the manner in which she held a book or soothed a pain, something that invited these questions and not others. Why ask her whether she was a child? She had talked about her childhood. She had told him of her sister. Everything, all there was, all that she could remember, she had said to him. What question was that and wherefore did it come, if he already knew?

It was in this crisscrossing, through this entanglement of the mind that she gained strength to carry on, to write more questions; strength to remember, to invent the memories of answers, to create more and more years. Strength to remain an answer. And even though she would not admit it, this strength, that which kept her drawing and writing and pacing around the room—this room inside of an apartment in a crowded city, or perhaps inside of a house overlooking the sea or a field of some kind; overlooking anything, really, for what does it matter where the room is as long as the door never opens—it was this strength that spoke to her as if it were a voice, that spoke of how unbreathable the air had become, how dense the ink on her hands and all around her, how heavy these lines and words and circles on the body; so heavy that it pinned her down and from then on she had to write in the most uncomfortable of positions; so heavy that she was beginning to feel nothing, no urge, no desire, nothing but this weight.

No desire, no need to keep going, from the very strength through which she went on, and on. No wish to remember, no warmth through the body. She was becoming cold under this inconceivable weight.

RUMMAGING THROUGH THE MIND in search of the perfect form to nonetheless carry on with her endeavor, even now, perhaps something resembling a final attempt, a paradoxical final attempt at the eternal, now when she herself feels as if she is dying, when she feels as if she is entering her final year, she thinks of the short poem—she thinks of the intensities and limitations of the short poem. Time dwindles and years pass. Years pass as she is lying there, writing under the weight of all that ink, of all those memories, under all those realities and errors and touches that have somehow come together and materialized atop of her; all of them, at once, the same weight that perhaps he was feeling, in her absence, when she was yet to become presence and heart in his life, the weight he was feeling when carrying around his neck all that life had given him and in which he told himself that he must find meaning. Years as if swept by the wind, years filled with the eternity she had created for herself, years brimming with the conventional togetherness she had respired life back into.

When I write, I take into myself all paradoxes. This is what she finds inside the mind. Paradoxes, losses, life burrowing deep into the soul and the spirit she no longer searches for on the canvas; she finds violent contradictions and ready-made analogies; she finds love and shocking claims at how to preserve this love. She finds memory and temporality. She finds pathologies and astonishing acts of living.

Years pass and exhaustion fills her body with more and more heaviness; years pass and exhaustion lays above her a blanket of ink—black and blue and red; vermillion; the red that returns from time to time to settle on her cheeks, when she cannot breathe, when the fingers no longer remember their impractical attempts at checking for a pulse. Years pass.

Years pass, and, exhausted by this perpetuity, surprised, even, that the eternal had proven to be such heavy a weight atop a body that needs lightness and movement and for her arms to have the pleasure of touching ample space as to write everything, everywhere, exhausted by all this, by the *always* and the *forever*, by the heights and depths of everything, she decides to uproot herself from the chaotic, from touch, from the *body of work*, from the body of newness, from desire, and from the senses themselves. From the stage and the theater and the night.

With a gesture of her left hand, she gives the page everything at once.

With a single gesture, within the passing of a second, less than a second, she floods the room with so many images, with so many instances of their loud voices, of their laughter and their cries; instances of their union, in echoes and movement and rustle of silk; with idealization, and instinct, and all that is bound up with their presence; with the carnal and the organic; with the blurring of distinction and with conventional living; with perception, and vocation, and all kinds of affirmations. She floods the room with so many questions, with so many answers; all of them. With a gesture of her left hand, she drowns, yes, she drowns the room and everything in it in organic matter that renders all communication impossible. There are now no ways through which the two humans living there might be able to reach for one another, no ways for two beings, the lonely ones, the *always-together* ones, the learning ones, no ways for them to grasp at nothing; nothing to do but to grasp for air in this sea of everything. This, in itself, a way for her to breathe. A way to say, Enough. An understanding of immortality not as possibility, but as weight atop the already exhausted body. A way to know that where he is, she too will be.

The scene is now inspired by life in a cathedral. His cathedral. The very first. A cathedral now in ruin, a cathedral where people live, where they seek shelter from the rain and the storm and, in winter, from snow that falls for too long and over too wide a stretch that nothing remains uncovered, nothing remains unfrozen. The cathedral is now a home. A home where to take shelter from the cold. Slightly to the left of her body, in a mirror, her reflection, or perhaps the reflection of someone who looks just like her, or, no, that very someone, holding a theater program between her knees, looking for something with which to light a fire. She is not alone there. How could she be? This cathedral, the very first, the last of the cathedrals, something for the eye to revel in, is where everyone in the world now lives. There, amidst so many bodies, she sees him. It is night, and none of them move, but nevertheless, she sees and recognizes him. No one moves, and yet, a step, another, and the space between them expands to unreal proportions, unbeknownst by the laws of physics, growing larger and larger with each attempt, with each breath and with each step, for now she can breathe, and, in this breathing, through this breathing, she brings into being all possible movements of the body. Of her body. Still, the image is not an accurate one. Still, they do not move. She lights the fire and lingers in its presence until warmth rushes through the veins.

All things can be made anew. There are ways. And if all things can be made anew, then so can all bodies, all living beings, all dying beings. There are ways.

When they arrived at the hospital, just days before the end, when for them it felt as if the end was going to come that very moment, on that cold morning when he gave in to her demands and agreed to put on clothes that hurt the skin, and take steps that hurt the body, and find himself there, where it hurt the soul—when they found themselves walking into the room where he would only spend a few hours, all she thought of was to find a way. To find a way not to fall there, that is, a way not to fall like some kind of plant that falls to the ground and dies even though its time has not yet come. And this, all the while she knew, of course, for he had said it before, to her and to himself—to her, as a means to make her let go, to him, as a means to hold on—his time had already passed.

On that day, when she thought of this, of everything, it felt as if it was something inherited, something abandoned on the floor as writing and as teachings by another version of herself, of themselves, by humans from other years and other lives; it felt already lived; used time, unkempt, messy, time that did nothing but exacerbate the problem, even when she felt as if this time stood still, even when time itself made it seem like that—for them and for them alone, there were now more hours, more days, more ways to live and to postpone the inevitable. She felt this, but her body, her mind, could not find ways to make from it anything other than a sensation on the skin, as if a gust of wind were gently passing through.

There, in the hospital room, all she managed to pull from the mind and turn into actual thought was how to find ways. Thought that constitutes something more than a tremor, something more than a fleeting sensation, thought she could hold and shape to her will. And little by little, these ways into not falling became ways into not forgetting and the ways into not forgetting became ways into not losing him, ways she had perhaps harbored in the mind for years and years, or the search for these ways, from the night she found herself across the corner from that small theater. Ways to keep him standing, even if it meant she would have to support him for all time. Ways to leave this place and return to their home. Ways to live there, together, even though she knew there might not be a next day. Ways to make the last day eternal. Ways aware of themselves. And so she planned. She hid from his gaze and drew and wrote and sketched what will become of life severed in half; and she did all this even though she did not yet know what her purpose was.

Her mind, her conscious mind, the mind through which she rummaged and the mind she made demands of, in moments of lucidity, that mind knew what was to become once he would no longer be a body and a soul and a part of the union of two beings who know not how to live in the world by themselves. But the day had not yet come, and hours later they left the hospital, promising themselves, promising him that no clothes will ever again hurt the skin, and no steps will ever again force the body to where the soul is in pain.

The pretext of the story remains the walk, the eternal walk, at night and in the daytime; the pretext remains this distancing of the real from the real.

If one were to look at them from afar, the living humans who once walked toward one another, close to midnight, denying all darkness; in a crowded city, on the beach, from opposite entries of the same tunnel; if someone were to direct their gaze and hold it there, on them, on her, on him, from afar, it would appear as if they were two silhouettes moving in opposite directions from one another. A curious thing. The distortion of this memory does not come from her writing. She has not placed it here herself, nor does she remember now very well how it came to be, how they came to be, it has faded, and there is no such walking, there is no walking toward one another, which means that there also is no moving apart, not even as metaphor, as poor a metaphor as it would be.

Unable to tell whether these silhouettes are of humans,

of animals, or of statues bestowed one night with movement, movement like that of living beings, by happenstance, for there are no miracles and there is no magic and if gods where to have their try, they would perhaps create more, they would do more, they would give more of a world for such statues, they would do more than make them abandon each other. They could perhaps make them break one another, violently, forcefully, with cruelty and lack of regret. They would make them break each other, a pause in time for each crack in the body of the statue, a moment to observe one's creation, for the gods. But yes, from afar, he and she, they appeared as if in the throes of separation.

The context that best emphasizes the image, however, is lacking. It is lacking from her, from him, and from their bodies when together. And so it is lacking from the spectator, and from whomever might gaze in their direction, and see them as statues breaking away from one another. It is lacking from their mind; it no longer passes through the brain that they will one day invent one for the other; it is lacking from whatever audience might be made possible when the text of the encounter is recreated, transferred, rather, from skin to page.

There is no context, yet they are but one body, and the distance between is nothing but that between a body and its shadow. In one sense, such distance does not even exist, while in another, the distance is the very thing that allows them to exist. One does not exclude the other. And it bears mentioning that there is no instance of the stage where a separation might even occur. She has filled it with so many objects, with so many paintings, with everything that she took from his neck, and from hers; with everything she took, little by little, from the necks of all the bodies in the world. She has brought it all here, so many pieces of furniture, so many trees, so many buildings in which to place apartments and narrow rooms. Everything is here, and so there is no space that might afford a separation. No manners of dismissal, nothing that can infiltrate, now, in the half-light, in the dark, nowhere. Nothing that can pass through the walls of their narrow room and create space for intima--cy to expand to the point of aloneness.

ON QUIET MORNINGS, when the sun pierces through the window at just the right angle, laying thus this necessary glow on her skin, as he reads something from the Homeric universe, something familiar to him by virtue of the little boy who looked up at the sky and read there all the books that he would ever feel the need to encounter; something that speaks of conditionings such as this one: the sun stroking her gently, as she sleeps, in their narrow room, much like the image of a verse, if verses were to all of a sudden become images before his eyes, if the poetic language of what resides in confrontation and in themselves, as bodies open to what nature might offer, were to materialize itself as this soft morning glow, as this light. A scene one surely understands by way of experience, of resemblance, of memory, even. The simplest memory there is: that of warmth from the sun.

On these mornings, comfortably, poignantly, and altogether marvelous, the aspiration toward perfection is no longer extant, and the length of their room makes no difference in how they encounter each other. This meta-morphic characteristic of reality is to accompany them throughout the day.

How do they resemble those of other years? How does this morning remain in spite of the gap between all things? In and out of space, in and out of time, the memory of this morning, like a crack that splits them asunder.

Later, she will refuse to cross the boundaries of this par-ticular morning. She will create for herself endless stretches of time, with the easiness with which one gets up from the chair and turns off the light, and in these stretches of time, she will linger only with this morning in mind, with this drive toward life; conventional life, stimulating life, day-to-day life, overflowing life; no longer distinguishing any-thing else, no longer recognizing, no longer desiring to find a path outside of it and cross it and find herself in the *beyond*, on the other side of life as she once knew it. In the course of this morning, in the reliving of this morning, the sun does not dry the skin, for there is so much sun, over and over again, that its presence becomes liquid and washes the body; the sun, always knowing how to find just the right angle for the glow it bestows to become the core and wonder of all days. Instead, from the glow that it places on her body, this glow like a shroud, the skin makes a kind of mist on which to feed, almost as if she is washing her body with pure air and emerging a new body from this trial. And again, inside her, endless stretches of time, where the room is not narrow, and if it is, it matters not; where the sky is never dark. And there, only there, always there, inside of time made to measure, where the mind thinks itself able to make this—to create time, time that does not end, time that holds but what pleases the mind, and the body, and the space that cradles them—there, she also finds a few other memories from their time together, memories she did not hold anywhere else, in any other time. For instance, memories of him leaving flowers on the dining room table, but it is not their table, and it is not their room, in fact, it is years before him, when she is barely twenty, when she has a dining room and a table just like that, but there are never flowers, for she never liked them. Flowers like a birthmark on a wooden body. Flowers like acts of divine creations. Flowers willing to touch skin with their petals; to touch skin and bestow upon the human not the glow of the sun, but the wetness of morning dew.

These memories that she finds there appear to her like small invasions. As if her life with him were seeping into all other lives. As if she had somehow managed to change not only the present, as if she had managed to create not only an eternal future, but also, somehow, the past. She never thought of it as an erasure. She never questioned these memories and whether they were in fact devouring

anything else; these false memories of a life unlived, con-
suming what had already passed, eating away, little by little,
at how she remembered herself, greedily gulping any other
face but his face, brushing away all other humans, all other
creatures, even—even all other trees and rivers and seas.
Though she dared not accuse these memories. No. She
held them tight. Tighter the more hours she spent in the
stretches of this pretend time. So tight that they would soon
become part of her body. Manifestations taking place in the
only *real* that needed to be real. So tight that soon her life
would become this unlived life the mind created in order
to give itself enough space, when it saw that the present,
that the future, no matter how eternal, provided no such
thing, when it saw that one can only find space, and possibility, and means of creating newness inside the past.

By the front door, a small note: What can one say?

It had been there for months. An invitation for phenomenology through the fingers. What can one say? What
can one do? Slipping, this thought, this question, as something to have a presence, as something to find oneself in
the presence of, without answering it, without addressing it
in any way other than acknowledging that it is there, that
it means something, that it will give birth to new meanings,
to new silences, to new ways of comfort. There, in the body
of the room, the desire for otherness. There, distance and

fragmentation as limbs of this body. There: faithfully, abundantly, lovingly. As image, as enigma, as reverberation through the body. An invitation from other worlds, other selves, other spaces; from the one who writes to the one who needs to be rewritten.

The note itself, the embodiment of this invitation, was perhaps written indeed by her, or him, or it could have been found in the street. A fortuitous act of walking. They could have found it on one of those streets that they used to cross, sometimes with reluctance, at night, in foreign cities, which neither of them had visited before; cities like well-run machineries, cities in the world like organs in the body; cobblestones of remembrance and linden fragrance and skin on which they might have written such small notes, such invitations to and from other realms.

To offer this note to the body of the narrow room: what inconceivable pleasure.

By then, they had both become intimately acquainted with these rituals of forgetting. In fact, there were at least five possibilities, although to offer a genuine depiction of them would be to erase their meaning; five paths that they would travel as to make forgetting happen, day after day, as to keep it from being forgotten itself. For what then would happen to the mind? Paths to lift the body, paths to illuminate awareness. Paths to make of the world a declaration of

togetherness. Paths taken when frantic or cruel or no longer in love, rituals that they had concocted and which served
their purpose admirably, in that final year, as most rituals do,
by preventing them from walking outside naked—outside,
where snow had yet to fall—undressed of everything that
protected the illusion of permanence. Rituals of erasure that
kept them from disappearing. That kept their union safe
from the blanket of snow to come. A doctrine, even, the
whole of these rituals, a form of expression that went
beyond themselves; an openness toward remaining hidden
within the narrow room. A correspondence to something
more fundamental, to the presence in the tomb of something territorial, something that would always remind him
that there was a narrow room, that there can only be this
narrow room. Something for her, something to let herself
be crushed under; a lineage; a rooting, of herself, in deaths
to come. Something to underscore not impossibility but its
very denial. An immortal *body of work*.

The whole of these rituals, a self-constituting conversation, one that perhaps provided no glimpse into the real
world, a conversation whose only purpose was to make the
other aware that, if constraints were to prevail, it would
only be in order for them to please one another, to prepare
their bodies for the arrival of multiple hearts, hearts that
could sustain endless lives; hearts like cobblestones, trans-
planted from one city into another. There would be no use,
otherwise, for their narrow room, no use for the walk at

night, no use for conjuring poets and making them trample on inside the pockets of the night, not for the sake of a survival metaphor.

Five paths. To depict them from beginning to end would be to erase their meaning, yet nevertheless paths they knew by heart, paths they have named and followed with the readiness of bodies that did not know how to live one with the erasure of the other. Five paths. The notes, the water, the return home, fig jam at six in the morning, disdain. Disdain not for themselves, but for the world, a method of conspiring against what had injured them, like a living, breathing organism, like a new person entirely, a new body, in the narrow room, assuming the same position as their own, mimicking their gestures, one by one; a reflection in the mirror, not of her, not of him, but of this unity, as they themselves have thought it: sublime and simple and possessive; worthwhile and obedient and in servitude of rituals that kept them from losing one another.

A dare. An extra hand. A touch, at great cost; a touch that could very well destroy the shape of things, out of respect for the world in which it had been created rather than for its creators; a hand that learns the same lessons they once did, a hand that bathes in the same stream they once did, when, as children, knew not of the other, but of the flow and rush toward a moment in which, without much trouble or concern, she would walk home along the city river, gazing at the darkness of the water, as if to conjure a memory of earlier time. When they knew not of the Other. When she was another child in the world. When he was the wandering eye.

A memory of the sky, passing by a small theater, close to midnight, when he, a willow, rooted there, in the most unusual of places, a willow to satisfy the stage, a willow at the mercy of the wind, suddenly and with lungs full of breath, with so loud a voice, loud enough for her to hear it, takes possession of any and all attempts at remembrance by recreating, for her and her alone, a model, perfection in a single breath, the breath before the very first breath together, a model of where they once lived even before living, a model of where they will be, of where they will find themselves and lose the world, of where she will perhaps live by herself, if she were to find her way back to where the rain falls, and from this rain, time births itself on the skin; to where she might love these raindrops caressing her like hours forever to come; if life were long, and linear, and knew how to preserve in the heart these wonders of planning one for the other: a narrow room, perhaps an armchair, perhaps a sense of comfort.

They have yet to be banished from this city of final hours. They have yet to find themselves swept into the eternal. An evocative imagery, a commentary on what is to come, something like that which one experiences in its own right, even though it never manifests itself, even though there is no aim, no search, no intention other than to speak of what has not yet come. An infinite conversation with the forces of life. With the forces of death. A conversation, when reversal occurs, and life becomes death, and death becomes life, and the *body of work* becomes the living body. They have yet to meet these limits. They have yet to comprehend their contradictions. They have yet to lose themselves, and through this loss, they have yet to become anachronism and time past. In a sense, they have yet to be. They have yet to walk the city at night. They have yet to encounter the theater. They are fastened one to the other, like phantoms, like adherences of flesh and bone, like thoughts coupled together, like literature and the one in need of it, like music and obscurity, like happy encounters and eternal reconciliations. The idea that they walk like this, on the shore, in the city, inside the narrow room, that they walk and share moments of conventional life and are aware of the oneday, this idea surpasses any others, and in doing so, it erases itself from their mind and from the collective mind, not of the world, but of themselves together, from the mind they have created as space, as togetherness, as space where to reach out and touch the Other, space in which the brushstroke and the word circle each other like small promises, on the floor, on the blue walls, beyond horizons and seas and skies as ways of beginning and endings. All versions of themselves: the real, the invented, the lonely ones.

They are fastened one to the other.

WHEN IT HAPPENED, WHEN DEATH CAME and everything ruptured, and, years from then, when her body was heavy with ink and her hands almost on the verge of nonwriting, the two of them were still to be banished from the city of final hours, they were still walking the streets of this city. In fact, at night, the city welcomed them and their doubles and the memory of other doubles, of other attempts; it welcomed them as if they were a depiction of its own nostalgia. The city welcomed her, and him, and their rituals, it approved of their seclusions toward one another, in spite of the world, toward that well-crafted routine, where notes were written so that real words could be erased from the mind; hurtful words, cruel words, words that would otherwise pierce through the representation of an image, of all images, words that would otherwise cut so deep that no rebirth would ever be possible. Words that would cut so deep and with such acerbic ardor that no stage could ever contain the bleeding. Instead, through these rituals, other words would come. Words that were written and read as explorations, of the world, of the skin, of the mind; words as traditions and dissociations from all tradition; fluid words, excessive words, words that to the outside world might have appeared barbaric, maddening. In the writing and reading of these new words, of all that comes and replaces separation, in the all-consuming blaze of these words, there, they are still walking the streets of the city.

Contrary to how she might have desired it, contrary to how she envisioned and planned it, life at the edge of the world was sometimes too carnal to be lived with ease. And other times, too allegorical to be fully grasped. Before, and after, and amid the events of their life together, something lingered at the root, a threat that spoke with a voice that she did not hear, a reference, a view, a nod to the purely biological life, to life how it courses through the veins of the living, through the memories of the dead, of life that exhausts and life that places one at crossroads, on thresholds, at the edge of all undesirable consequences. She was more aware of this life when she was tired. Infinitely tired, with exhaustion seeping to and from the brain; exhaustion like deconstruction, exhaustion like love lost, exhaustion like a reality that, even though no longer mysterious, remained hidden and unwelcomed. Then, life came to her as a kind of third realm, as a possibility that she would only encounter when half-asleep, when struggling not to give in to the erasure of the mind. In those moments, it was as if she were living another life. Her memories were others, her thoughts, and gestures and even her echoes were others. Whenever it came, this life, it came with the same presence, it held within the same events, time after time, truly as if it were a third existence, a continuity that depended on exhaustion to manifest itself. A continuity always between sleep and wakefulness, always when the mind was too entangled in the threads of satisfaction, and conclusion, and the need for eternity. Always, this continuity, always, this life, always the same memories; not her memories, not his, not of anyone she ever encountered. When this life manifested itself upon the eyelids, when she was on this threshold, it was as if another *here* and another *her* were brought into existence, another but not altogether different. And she lived this life, when tired, when struggling with sleep, when ascending and descending, she lived it as she would have lived any other life. She gave herself to this life, she learned its gestures, she unified its timelines, she became herself the embodiment of the desires of this life. The bitterest pleasure and the sweetest pain of this life. And when she was aware of it, in those few seconds before it took over, though there was always a kind of veil, there was always something like a second skin, something manifesting itself alongside this life, the realization that it is not her life, that she is not awake but that she is not asleep either —when she was aware of it, what most wounded her was the forgetting. Yes, the forgetting, for she could not accept that this is newness, that this life was something she had birthed alongside the two humans, the recreated ones; she denied any and all reasonings of the mind that would hint at this third way of living as something born from the heaviness of ink, from the exhaustion of eternal togetherness. And so, she was wounded by the forgetting of this life. Wounded by never having sensed it throughout their conventional life together. Of never having asked him whether he felt and lived it too. Whether there was life behind his eyelids when not asleep, when not awake, when on the threshold, and if so, whether this life was the same as hers.

When death came, this life was nothing but a possibility, though one could not call it such, rather, an unknown, but an unknown that no one thinks of, a primal existence beyond all existences; something waiting, lingering, something deepening the abyss of itself, until, one day, it would climb from there and settle under the eyelids, until, one day, it would come and become ecstasy, and horror, and the nothingness of death as seen by the eye, as felt by the skin, as written and then erased from the text by the hand. She will recall this life for years to come. She will make herself seek this life. She will bring herself to the point of exhaustion enough as to reveal that threshold, enough as to be capable of manifesting this life. Her only explanation, her only thought: this is a life as eternal as the one she has created for her, for him, yet an eternity that is given to her by something exterior, and thus not dependent on her writing hand, not dependent on her own existence. This is why she seeks this life, as continuity beyond all deaths. As last word that will never be erased, as last word that will never be forgotten, as last word that grows and grows and from it whole sentences, whole pages, whole other lives are born. Having the possibility of this last word, of this third realm under the eyelids, upon the threshold between sleep and wakefulness, having this, she feels lighter, but only for a moment.

If an image were to be attempted, an image of an after-death, an image of the future, an image like a vision granted both to the living and the dead, it would perhaps be this: the image of her body as she writes, growing heavier and heavier, with ink, with the unbreathable air that nonetheless fills her lungs, the air that fills the room whose door never opens. It would be an image like a suffocating embrace, the image of years passing in this heaviness, with the hand no longer knowing how to follow the line of the face, no longer knowing how to do anything but keep alive this conventional life that she did not have enough strength to let wither. It would be the image of lines and circles and words creating themselves, and from themselves, creating him, and her; another *her*, another *him*; creating them, night after night, morning after morning. The image of two lovers eternally in the throes of creation. Never resting, never sleeping, never without breath. The image of two lovers, living longer, living eternally.

If an image where to be needed, desired, attempted, manifested, it would also be the image of one day pausing; a break, a stop in time as to find something, no, to find herself broken under so much weight; an image of flooding the room with everything at once, with everything that two humans, the lonely ones, the invented ones, would need in order to survive in the absence of her writing hand.

If an image of the future were to become an image of the present, an image of all times and for all times, an interpretation of time itself, it would be this: the door of the narrow room opening, and with it, through it, forgetting that comes and drowns the mind of the one who writes, of the one who once wrote, for now she would be traveling, now she would go in search of a small house to rent, in search of filling other walls, not with photographs, but with hours of writing letters to someone she would no longer remember. A narrow room, an armchair, a measure of comfort, however short the time.

Night opens its pockets and frees from there anything and anyone; night opens its pockets and releases whomever fell for the trap of its protection. A kindness beyond the possibility of darkness. A kindness that one could only encounter in darkness. A kindness bestowed by the blue night, the night outside their window, the night outside of all windows; night like day, night like threshold, night like what is moving gently toward dawn, night waiting; night always waiting, for her hand to write a path for its stars and for its dreams, even, perhaps, waiting for her to draw the very windows it is to force open. Night that comes into being through the gesture of the body. Of bodies, together, bodies, next to one another, bodies walking the length of time, bodies on stage, bodies dwelling among the eternal.

When death came, when self-surrender came and took hold of his eyes, of the tremor of his hands, when what preserved a final instance of life was slowly fading to the point of nonbeing, in the reception of this coming, there remained the necessary glow of the skin, the blue murals of childhood, the infinite distance, and the essence of touch. In all this, through all this, in this moment that she no longer remembers, and even if she were to remember, she would never write of it, so that it would not become a memory for them, in this, in the time when perhaps one was meant to whisper, There is no Other. Then, what remained was death as a possibility for new life.

Death as life through the *body of work*, through the body of the Other as writing and reinvention, as reiteration and actualization of all spirits and souls and divinities. To consider what such a love entailed, at the end, in the beginning, when possibilities abound and lives come now as shadows of the body, of the only body able and capable of maintaining them, to think then of why this love, of why these chapters, of why these hands, the film-projecting hands, the writing hands, the hands on the threshold of new life: an inconceivable act.

Significant and always excessive, adoring and always ardent, the never-enough, the plea for eternity, for the body to remain body, for the mind to remain mind, for the hand to paint, and write, and make of days and of nights a memory, a newness, a language.

Inside the narrow room, films are now projected on all walls, and in the corners, she has placed enough ink so as to never be without the possibility of writing.

Outside, the first snow of the year falls with the impatience of a theater curtain awaiting its next representation. Worlds away, sky and sea become indistinguishable from one another. Not by virtue of color, not by reverberation, not by anything that one might be able to define or portray in any way.

Unnamed, this: sea and sky, dissolving into each other, separated but fused together. Landscape and the urge for new paths to be created; landscape and the desire of the wandering eye to see what it would most please it, to make for itself what it needs in order to keep roving, in order to remain, this eye, to remain the map and the journey and the time that will allow their coming together.

Sky and sea; one blue, the other blue, distinct yet dissolving into one another; sky, and sea, and the never-enough; the brushstroke of language and the ink of paintings as correspondences between worlds, between realms; as the gap between all things. This gap, ever-engulfing, the blue at the feet of all things, the blue on the hands of all beings, of all variations of the self, the blue on the body of all deaths. Sea and sky. Two humans. The lonely ones. The only ones. His hand in the color of her body.

On the floor, she writes: In the half-light, in the dark, nowhere. Later, he will ask her his December question.

This book is a letter, a gesture of boundless love and gratitude, a tribute to Edvard Munch, who in his journals wrote: "I felt the greatest pleasure in knowing that I would be returning to this earth—this always fermenting earth—always to be shone upon by the living sun—alive. I would be at one with it—and out of my rotting corpse would grow plants and trees and grass and plants and flowers and the sun would warm them and I would be a part of them and nothing would perish—that is eternity." (tr. Jennifer Lloyd), and whose paintings have offered the marvelous backcloth of blue and separation into which I have weaved this story.

# About the Author

Christina Tudor-Sideri is a writer and translator. She is the author of the book-length essay *Under the Sign of the Labyrinth*, the novel *Disembodied*, and the collection of fragments, *If I Had Not Seen Their Sleeping Faces*. Her translations include works by Max Blecher, Magda Isanos, Anna de Noailles, Mihail Sebastian, and Ilarie Voronca.

# ALSO FROM SUBLUNARY EDITIONS